FORD

SUPERMODELS
OF THE WORLD™

THE
NEW
ME

"Who is this?" I asked, pressing the telephone receiver closer to my ear.

"Let me start again," said the voice on the other end of the line. "My name is Jill Murray. I'm calling from Ford Models in New York City. I'd like to speak to Paige Sanders."

"This is Paige," I answered, tracing my finger along the red checked pattern of the tablecloth. "But I still don't understand..."

"Well, Paige," said Jill Murray, "we received your photo here at the agency..."

"My photo?"

"Oh," she said, "maybe you aren't the right Paige Sanders. I am calling Wheeler, Nebraska, aren't I?"

"Yes," I said, nodding even though she couldn't see me.

"And did you send in a photograph to Ford Models in New York City?" Jill asked.

"I don't think so," I said. Then I realized what she must be talking about. "Oh my gosh— Nana!"

"Nana?" she repeated.

"Um, yeah, that's my grandmother," I explained. "She must be the one who sent in my picture. She's always telling me I should model."

"Well, then, I'd say your grandmother has a great eye," said Jill. She laughed. "Let me explain. Eileen and Jerry Ford are very impressed by your photo. They think you've got real potential. And they're usually right. They'd like you to come to New York as soon as possible for test photos."

"To New York?" I repeated. "You mean New York City?" I stood up and walked over to the sink in a daze. I couldn't believe my ears.

"That's right," said Jill. "And if the photos turn out well, it's very likely that Ford will want to sign you on as one of their models."

"Oh my gosh," I said. I gripped the edge of the sink until my knuckles turned white. Maybe I was dreaming. Was it really possible that this was true? I thought this kind of thing only happened in the movies.

"Of course, Ford will make all the arrangements for your visit to New York," Jill went on. "You know, setting you up with the photographers, finding you a place to stay and everything."

As she went into more details I stared at the window over the kitchen sink. There was my reflection, the same as always—the same long, curly red hair, the same tortoise-shell glasses. But was this actually happening to me? My grandmother had always told me I should think about modeling, but I had never really taken her seriously. I mean, grandmothers are supposed to think you're beautiful.

Then Jill said something that brought me back to down to earth fast.

"And Eileen will be happy to talk to your parents about it before you come, to set their minds at ease and let them know that you'll be in good hands in New York."

"Oh," I said. "My parents…"

My eyes refocused beyond my own reflection in the window onto the yard and the cornfield. I could see my mother taking the laundry from the clothesline and my father in the distance, beside our red tractor.

My parents—how was I ever going to convince them to let me, their fifteen-year-old daughter, leave Wheeler, Nebraska, to go to New York and be a model?

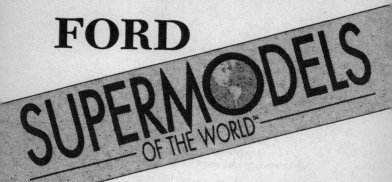

FORD
SUPERMODELS
OF THE WORLD™

THE
NEW
ME

by B. B. Calhoun
based on a concept by Liz Nickles

RED FOX

Created by R. R. Goldsmith

A Red Fox Book

Published by Random House Children's Books
20 Vauxhall Bridge Road, London SW1V 2SA

A division of Random House UK Ltd
London Melbourne Sydney Auckland
Johannesburg and agencies throughout the world

3 5 7 9 10 8 6 4 2

First published in the United States by
Random House, Inc 1994

SUPERMODELS OF THE WORLD is a trademark of
Ford Models Inc.

Printed and bound in Great Britain by
Cox & Wyman Ltd, Reading, Berkshire

RANDOM HOUSE UK Limited Reg. No. 954009

ISBN 0 09 955301 5

The FORD SUPERMODELS OF THE WORLD™
series . . . collect them all!

Enter a world of glamour, high fashion and fun
with six aspiring young supermodels: Paige,
Cassandra, Naira, Kerri, Katerina and Pia!

Now available:
      1. The New Me
      2. Party Girl
And coming soon:
      3. Having It All
      4. Making Waves
      5. Stepping Out
      6. High Style

CONTENTS

Chapter 1	1
Chapter 2	12
Chapter 3	24
Chapter 4	43
Chapter 5	56
Chapter 6	78
Chapter 7	87
Chapter 8	101
Chapter 9	115
Chapter 10	126
Chapter 11	141
Chapter 12	153
Chapter 13	163

CHAPTER 1

"I don't know, Paige," Dad said at dinner the next night. "New York is a pretty dangerous place."

"Oh, don't be silly, Dan," said my grandmother. She heaped mashed potatoes onto her plate, then passed them across the long kitchen table. "Now you know that the Fords have promised she'll be well looked after while she's there. Why, you talked to Eileen Ford yourself. Besides, they do this sort of thing with young girls all the time. I read all about it in one of those articles in *Teen Scene* magazine."

"Nana," cried Erin, my thirteen-year-old sister, "you've been taking my magazines out of my room again!"

"Oh hush, Erin," said Nana, pouring gravy on her potatoes. "I'm not doing your maga-

1

zines any harm. Besides, if I hadn't seen that article on the Fords and sent in Paige's picture, she would never have had this opportunity."

"Well, it isn't fair," said Erin. She put down her fork and folded her arms over her chest. "It was *my* magazine. *I* should get to go to New York, too."

People have always said that Erin and I look alike. It's true that we both have my mother's red hair, but I'm the tall one, like Dad. Erin's petite like Mom, which guys seem to like a lot, but she's way too short to model.

The funny thing was, I'd always wished that I was small and delicate like Erin and Mom. This was the first time that I'd ever thought there might actually be something good about being tall.

"Hey, if Paige goes, can I have her room?" asked my eleven-year-old brother, Danny, with a mouthful of food.

"All right, everyone, that's enough," Mom said firmly. "No one is going to New York—at least, not right now. Paige can't possibly think of going anywhere with school starting in just a couple of weeks."

Suddenly, I couldn't take it any more. I felt

2

like everyone was deciding my future without even *asking* me what *I* wanted.

"Does anyone mind if *I* have an opinion about all this?" I blurted out.

Everyone stopped eating and looked at me.

"Of course not, honey," said Mom, her face softening. "Go ahead, tell us what you think."

"Well," I said, taking a deep breath, "I've been doing a lot of thinking since Jill Murray called. It's all happened so quickly and I know that New York is really far away. Believe me, the whole idea kind of scares me. But, you know, this a chance most people never get. If I don't take it I might be sorry for the rest of my life."

"But sweetheart," said Mom, "what about school?"

"The Fords said that this visit would be just to test me," I said. "They just want to get some professional pictures taken to see if I'm any good at modeling at all, which I may not be. And I also think it will be a chance for me to try *them* out, too—and New York and modeling. If I'm not good at it or I hate it, I'd probably be back in time for school."

"What if you do like it, and the Fords offer to take you on?" Mom asked.

"Well, I answered, "*if* that did happen, and *if* it was okay with you all, then the Fords would set me up in a school there, like they said." I was trying hard to sound sure of myself. But as I looked around our kitchen at the yellow cabinets, the red checked curtains on the windows, and all the other familiar sights I had grown up with, I couldn't imagine feeling at home anywhere else.

Dad shook his head. "I can't see it," he said. "My little girl all alone in New York City. It doesn't seem to me like it's the right place for a kid."

"Oh, nonsense, Dan," said Nana. "Plenty of kids grow up there and turn out just fine. Besides, our Paige has a good Wheeler, Nebraska, upbringing." She winked at me. "I know you'll be the best model they ever saw in New York, Paige."

"Thanks, Nana," I said. I smiled at her. I was really excited, but I still couldn't help wishing that I felt as confident as my grandmother did about the whole thing.

Two days later I sat on the floor of my room, my suitcase open on the pink-and-blue rag rug that Nana had made me when I was little.

Clothes were everywhere, and my cat, Scooter, lay curled up in the middle of it all. My two best friends, Laura and Kim, sat on my bed with its ruffled pink-and-white checked comforter.

"There's no way you can take all that stuff with you, Paige," Laura said, her dark ponytail swinging as she shook her head.

"I know, I know," I said. "I just can't figure out what I should pack."

"Well, you'd better decide soon," said Laura with a grin. "You're leaving tomorrow."

"I bet New York will be totally glamorous," said Kim. She piled all of her straight blond hair on top of her head and sucked in her cheeks, in an attempt to look glamorous herself. "You shouldn't take anything that makes you look like you're from Nebraska."

"Now how's she supposed to do that?" asked Laura, shaking her head. "She *is* from Nebraska. And anyway, what's so wrong with Nebraska?"

"I just mean that she should try to look a little more sophisticated," said Kim. She let her hair fall to her shoulders and picked up a magazine from the nightstand next to my bed and began leafing through it. "You know, more hip, more cool, more like *this*."

I looked at the page she held up. It showed a photograph of a model with short, jet black hair. Her face was powdered almost white, and she was wearing dark eye makeup and purplish lipstick. She had on a long, slinky black dress and purple high-top sneakers.

"Gee, I guess this is out of the question, then," I said, holding up a white cotton dress with little yellow flowers on it and heart-shaped buttons down the front.

"Absolutely out of the question," said Kim. "You can't wear something like that in New York. You'll look like a total hick."

I put the dress down. It had always been one of my favorites, but Kim was probably right. I couldn't walk around New York City looking like I had just stepped off a farm, even if I really *had*.

"You won't forget about all of us back here in Wheeler when you become a famous model, will you, Paige?" asked Laura.

"Are you kidding?" said Kim. "If it were me, I'd want to erase this boring little town from my memory as soon as I got there."

"Look, guys, the way I see it, I'll probably be back in time to start school with you," I said. "After all, tons of girls want to be models, but only a few ever really make it."

"Don't worry, Paige," said Laura. "You'll be one of them."

"Yeah," said Kim. "I've got a feeling you'll be a big success in New York."

"Well," I said, feeling a lump form in my throat as I reached out to scratch Scooter behind the ears, "either way, I promise I'll never ever forget you guys or Wheeler."

That night, as my family was finishing dinner, there was a knock at the door.

"It's me," said the voice of ten-year-old Pete Nelson. The Nelsons owned the farm down the road. My brother, sister, and I had always played with the Nelson kids—Pete, Brian, Scott, and Tommy.

"Hi, everybody," said Pete as he walked in, as comfortable as if he were family. "Can Danny come out and hit some softballs with me and my brothers behind the barn?"

"You may be excused from the table, Danny," Dad said.

"Great," said my brother, pushing back his chair. "I'll go get my mitt."

I looked past Pete, through the screen door

to the Nelsons' barn in the distance. The sun was just beginning to go down, and the sky had this beautiful orange gold glow. It reminded me of all the nights that Erin, Danny, and I had played outside after dinner with the Nelsons. Then I knew that was just where I wanted to spend my last night in Wheeler.

"I'll come, too," I told Pete.

"Are you all finished with your packing, Paige?" Mom asked.

"We have to leave for the airport bright and early, you know," said Dad.

"I'll be ready." I pushed back my chair. "Hey, Danny," I called, "bring my glove, too!"

"Mine, too," cried Erin, jumping up to follow me.

"Come back in when it gets dark," said Mom. "Bring the boys, and you can all have some ice cream."

Danny, Erin, Pete, and I walked over toward the Nelsons' barn. I felt better than I had in days. I knew I was really going to miss my family, but I was about to set off on an incredible adventure. I'd never been out of Nebraska before in my life. And tomorrow I would leave to be in a totally new place. I was going to meet new people and maybe even start an amazing career. The whole thought of it still made me feel out of breath.

Near the barn I could see Tommy Nelson batting as his brother Brian pitched to him. Tommy was sixteen, the oldest of the Nelsons, and a year older than I. I'd known him for as long as I could remember. We'd been best friends when we were little—swimming in the pond together in the summers, having snowball fights in the winters, and once, when we were eight, getting in big trouble for hiding in the Nelsons' hayloft while our parents searched all over both farms trying to find us.

Lately I'd been looking at Tommy in a new way, noticing different things about him. Like the way he shook his sandy hair off his forehead. And how his blue eyes wrinkled at the corners when he smiled. He'd also really filled out this past year. I watched his strong shoulders move under his white T-shirt as he swung the bat, and I couldn't help getting a fluttery feeling inside.

"Hey," he said, as we walked up. He grinned at me. "Carrot Top! You playing?"

"Sure," I said. I felt my cheeks flush at his old nickname for me.

We decided the positions and the order. I was first to bat, so I pushed my glasses up on my nose and stepped up to the plate. It made me feel so alive to be out there, swinging the bat and seeing the lights of my own house glowing in the distance.

Finally, the sun went down behind the cornfield, and the only light in the sky was a thin purple streak.

"We'd better get back," I said. "My mom says you guys can all come over for ice cream if you want."

"Great," said Brian.

"Last one there is a rotten egg!" called Danny. He, Erin, Pete, Brian, and Scott took off toward the house.

"Danny! You forgot your glove!" I called, but they were already out of earshot.

Shaking his head, Tommy bent down to pick up the glove and tossed it to me.

"What are they going to do without you?" he asked.

I shrugged. Everything with the Fords had happened so fast that I hadn't had a chance to tell Tommy I was going, but I knew his mother must have told him. Mrs. Nelson and my mom talked every day.

"I might be back in less than two weeks," I said.

"And you might not," he replied. His blue eyes gazed at me through the purple light.

"Yeah, um, I guess," I said. I shrugged and looked at my sneakers.

Suddenly I felt Tommy's hand on my chin, tilting my face up toward his.

"I'm going to miss you, Carrot Top," he said quietly.

"I'll miss you, too, Tommy," I said, my own voice shaking a little.

The next thing I knew, his face was moving closer to mine. I closed my eyes and felt our lips touch. My first thought was how strange it all was. Nothing like this had ever happened between Tommy and me before. But then the whole thing felt completely normal, almost as if I'd known this moment would come since we were little kids.

As Tommy let go of my chin, I opened my eyes and saw him smiling at me.

"Come on, Carrot Top," he said, grinning mischievously. "Last one back is a rotten egg!"

I grinned back, and we both took off across the grass as fast as we could toward the house in the distance.

CHAPTER 2

"Ladies and gentlemen, we will begin our descent into New York in approximately ten minutes," said the flight attendant's voice. "Please fasten your seat belts."

I sat up straight, buckled my seat belt, and leaned over toward the window. What I saw in the distance made me gasp. There it was—the New York City skyline, just like it looked in all the pictures, a jagged row of tall gray buildings outlined against the blue sky. I pressed my nose to the window, trying to get a better view.

I thought about my family back at the farm. Right about now, they would be finishing lunch. I imagined my dad heading back out to do the afternoon chores, with Erin and Danny along to help him. I saw my mom clearing the table, Scooter following her into

the kitchen, winding around her legs and meowing for scraps.

I wondered what Tommy was doing right
now. It was hard to sort out my feelings about
him after what had happened between us. I
had written all about it in my diary the night
before, but I still wasn't sure how I felt. I wondered if he looked at our friendship different-
ly now. I mean, it wasn't like that one kiss
suddenly made us boyfriend and girlfriend or
anything, but it had changed things a little, at
least in my mind.

Then I saw the runway directly below. A
moment later the wheels of the plane touched
the ground. A shiver of excitement went
through me as the pilot announced that we'd
arrived in New York City. I couldn't believe it.
I was actually here!

I followed the line of passengers off the
plane and down a long hallway. I pushed up
my glasses and tucked stray curls of hair behind my ear. Then I tried to smooth the wrin-
kles out of the big white shirt I had taken
from my dad's closet that morning to wear
with my black leggings and flowered vest.
Someone from Ford was supposed to meet
me, and I hoped I looked all right.

The hallway opened onto a larger room where a crowd of people waited behind a low metal partition. I noticed a small white cardboard sign waving in the air above the crowd. Printed on it in black marker was my last name. As I got closer I could see a short, pretty woman holding the sign above her head. She wore jeans and a green sweater and looked about twenty-five. Her straight auburn hair was pulled into a ponytail.

"Paige?" she asked as I walked toward her.

"Yes," I said, smiling nervously.

"Hi, how are you?" she said. She smiled back at me and shook my hand. "I'm Carla Harris from Ford. Now, let's see, the driver's waiting outside with the car. But you probably have lots of luggage to get first, right?" She took my arm and began to lead me through the crowd. "Here, let me take that bag for you. How was your flight?"

"Fine," I told her. "Great."

I was relieved to be with Carla as we made our way through the airport. It seemed huge, much bigger than the airport in Omaha where the plane had taken off from. People were rushing in every direction, but Carla seemed to know just where she was going.

After we picked up my two suitcases, Carla led me out of the airport and right up to a large black car. I couldn't help being impressed when a driver stepped out and opened the trunk for my bags. The car wasn't one of those fancy limousines that celebrities ride around in, but it was more like a limo than any car that I'd ever been in before.

Carla and I slid into the back seat, and the driver took his place up front.

"We're going to Ford first," Carla told me, as the car pulled out of the airport. "We'll get you checked in there, then I'll take you to where you'll be staying."

"Okay," I said. I hoped I didn't look like too much of a wreck. Ford had said they'd arrange for me to stay in a room in an apartment with some other models. I wished we could stop by there first so I could wash up and brush my hair.

I could see the city skyline in the distance as we drove along the highway. It was hard to believe that this was the place that was going to be my home for at least the next twelve days—maybe longer.

Twenty minutes later, we pulled off the highway and onto a bridge.

"That's the East River," Carla told me, as I looked down at the sparkling strip of water.

"And *that*?" I asked, pointing out the window at something that looked like a tiny red train car. It was hanging high above the river, moving along what looked like a thick telephone line.

"Oh, that's the tram," said Carla. "It goes to Roosevelt Island, which is in the middle of the river. People who live there commute on the tram."

"You mean that's how they get home?" I asked, amazed.

"Sure," said Carla. "Lots of people take the tram to work and back every day."

I shook my head. Somehow, I just couldn't imagine dangling above the water in that little red car every day. There must not be many people in New York who are afraid of heights, I decided, gazing from the tram to the tall buildings up ahead.

The bridge came to an end, and the car turned onto a busy street. Finally, we came to a stop in front of a narrow, red brick, four-story building with a pair of double doors painted black. A sign above the big, plate-glass window on the ground floor said FORD MODELS INC.

I felt a shiver go through my body.

"Well, here we are," said Carla.

We walked into the building and through a small reception area, where we left my suitcases. Carla led me up a flight of stairs to the second floor and into a room where a young woman with short dark hair sat behind a desk.

"Jill, this is Paige Sanders," Carla said. "Paige, Jill Murray."

Jill's face lit up. "Paige, hi. Welcome to New Model Development. Have a seat."

"Thanks," I said. I sat down in the chair in front of her desk.

"The first thing we're going to do is get some information on you," said Jill.

"I've got some things to do. I'll be back to get you in a little while, Paige," said Carla, heading for the stairs.

"Okay, thanks," I said. I turned to Jill. "What kind of stuff do you want to know?"

"Well, of course height, weight, hair color, eye color, and your shoe and clothing sizes," said Jill. She picked up a stack of papers on her desk and handed them to me. "But we also want to know about your hobbies and interests, you know, any particular skills and talents you may have. Like gymnastics, or water skiing, for example."

"Well," I said, thinking, "I ride horses."

"Perfect," said Jill. "That's just the kind of thing we're looking for." She handed me a pen. "Be sure to put that down. Then if we get a request for a girl of your physical description who can horseback ride, we can send you out for the job."

"I get it," I said, nodding.

I began filling out the forms. Some of the questions were easy—name, age, place of birth, and stuff like that. Then there were a lot of questions about physical appearance. But the hard ones to answer were about hobbies and talents. I put down horseback riding under "Special Talents," but there were a few other questions that I felt like I didn't have answers for, at least not very good ones.

For example, there was a section called "Languages Spoken." True, I'd taken French at Wheeler High, but I wouldn't exactly say I could speak it. In fact, I kind of doubted if I could even carry on a simple conversation with a real French person. So I ended up just putting English.

Then there were a few other sections that asked for things like "Theatrical Background" and "Dance/Movement Training." I'd never really done anything like that at all. In fact, as the forms went on, I began to worry that I didn't have *any* talents that Ford Models would be interested in. Not that I didn't have certain kinds of special training in *some* areas, but there weren't exactly any places on the forms to write in stuff like "driving a tractor" and "baling hay."

"Great," said Jill, taking the papers when I was finished. "Now, I'll just let Eileen know that you're here." She picked up the phone.

"Eileen Ford?" I asked. "You mean I'm going to meet her now?"

Jill smiled. "Why, yes. Eileen likes to get to know all the girls personally."

Oh no, I thought. I knew I looked terrible after that long flight. Just my luck, having to meet the head of Ford Models looking like this. Quickly I smoothed down my hair.

"She says to go right in," said Jill, waving toward a door behind her.

I gently pushed open the door and peered

inside. Sitting behind a big, pale wooden desk was a small woman with short light hair and glasses. Spread out on the desk in front of her were photographs of models. Eileen Ford looked up and gave me a big smile.

"Well, hello," she said. "You must be Paige. Welcome, welcome."

"Hi, Mrs. Ford," I said. "It's really nice to meet you."

"It's wonderful to meet you, too, Paige," she said. She walked around from behind her desk. "And please, call me Eileen. All of our models do. Now, come on in and sit down. Would you like a cup of tea?"

"Um, okay, Mrs. F—I mean, Eileen," I said. "Thank you."

She led me to a small flowered couch at the opposite end of the room. On a low table in front of it was a beautiful pink-and-white tea pot with two matching cups.

"You must be exhausted from your flight," Eileen said. She sat down on the couch and patted the cushion next to her. "I find that almond tea is very rejuvenating after a long trip."

I sat down as she poured the tea and handed me a cup. Looking around the room, I was amazed by what I saw. I loved it right away. It wasn't anything like what I had expected the office of the head of New York's top model agency to look like. In fact, the whole room seemed more like a cozy place in the country. Most of the furniture was made out of a light wood, and the couch and chairs were covered with calico cushions. I wished my father could see me sitting there. The place was so homey, and Eileen was so nice, I knew it would make him feel better right away about my being in New York.

Eileen asked me about my family, so I told her about the farm and my parents, and about Erin and Danny and Nana and even Scooter. I couldn't get over how easy she was to talk to.

Believe it or not, the person that I decided Eileen Ford reminded me of was the head librarian at the Wheeler Library, Mrs. Johnson. Mrs. Johnson was tough about things like library rules and overdue books, and a lot of kids were kind of scared of her. But she had always liked me, probably because I read so much. And I could see her soft side when she talked about a book she really loved or when she read out loud to a group of little kids in the Children's Room. I got the feeling that Eileen was like that, too.

"Well," said Eileen, as I finished my tea, "I suppose you must be anxious to go and get settled in. Let me tell you a little bit about where you'll be staying. Five other models, who are around your age and who are also new to New York, are staying there. As I explained to your parents on the telephone, Mrs. Hill will be the housemother in residence and the guardian of all you girls. So listen to her advice and follow her rules while you're here."

"Okay," I said, nodding.

"Now, Jill will be in touch with you to let you know about any appointments she sets up," Eileen went on. "You should be ready to work at all times. That means being well groomed, showing up for shoots with clean hair and nails, and no makeup. We'd also like you to avoid sun tanning. Remember, you never know when we might schedule you to do a test with a photographer or even a booking."

"A booking?" I repeated, not sure what she meant.

"A job," Eileen explained. "Since you haven't worked before, our first important

22

step will be developing your book. This is your portfolio of photographs, which gets shown to anyone who might be interested in working with you."

"I get it," I said. Suddenly it seemed like there were a lot of new things to remember. I hoped I would be able to keep it all straight.

"Welcome to New York, Paige," said Eileen with a smile. "I'm sure you're going to do very well here." She stood up. "Now, let's see if we can find Carla to take you over to the apartment so you can settle in and make yourself at home."

"Thanks," I said. But somehow, as I thought of the busy streets and bustling people outside, I couldn't imagine this place ever really being like home to me. In fact, I was starting to feel like I had left Wheeler, Nebraska, for a completely different planet!

CHAPTER 3

I stood on the tenth floor of the apartment building where Carla had dropped me off and rang the doorbell of apartment 10-B.

A girl with long brown hair opened the door and broke into a huge smile. She was wearing the most amazing vest I'd ever seen. It was covered with buttons of different sizes and colors.

"*Ciao*, hi! Katerina?" she said, raising her eyebrows.

"Uh—no," I said. I hoped I didn't have the wrong door. I was sure that Carla had said to go to 10-B, though. And this girl definitely looked like a model. Not only did she have gorgeous hair, she had a really pretty face with bright blue eyes. And she was tall, maybe even taller than me, but that could have been the funky platform shoes she had on.

24

"Ah, *peccato*, that's too bad," said the girl. She pouted a little, then looked back at me and smiled. "I'm sorry, please come in. I do not mean to be rude. It's just that I thought you might be Katerina, the girl who will share my room. I have been waiting to meet her." She pointed to my two suitcases. "These are yours, no?"

"No—I mean yes," I answered.

"I am Pia," said the girl. She picked up the biggest of my two bags. "Pia Giovanni. From Italy."

"Hi, Pia," I said, grabbing the second bag. "I'm Paige Sanders, from Nebraska."

"Nebraska, that is one of the United States, no?" she asked, dragging the heavy bag inside.

"Yes, that's right," I answered. At first it seemed like kind of a funny question. But when I thought about it I realized that I wasn't exactly an expert on the geography of Italy, either.

I followed Pia into the apartment and looked around the large living room. The far wall had a big window in it, and outside you could see the river. Under the window were two huge white armchairs that looked really comfortable and a glass coffee table. A matching white couch stood against another wall.

A very pretty girl with a straight blond ponytail was lying on her back on the white rug, somehow managing to talk on the telephone and do leg lifts at the same time. She had on a turquoise-and-white striped T-shirt and a pair of black bicycle shorts. She looked like she belonged on a beach in California. I wondered how she felt about the no-tanning rule.

Pia dropped my bag on the floor. The blond girl looked up and waved at us but kept talking into the receiver. I wondered how she managed to count her leg lifts, but then again she looked like she could do them all day and not break a sweat.

"*Signora* Hill!" Pia called loudly. "Paige from Nebraska is here!"

A heavyset woman with short curly blond hair walked into the room. I'd been worried that Mrs. Hill was going to be stylish and intimidating. But after sitting in Eileen Ford's office, I should have known she'd pick the right person for the job. Mrs. Hill, wearing brown pants and a simple blouse, was wiping her hands on a dish towel and smiling at me, just like my mom or Mrs. Nelson would have done. I couldn't help but smile back.

"Hello, hello," she said. "Welcome. I'm Mrs. Hill."

"Hi, I'm Paige Sanders," I answered.

"Paige, of course, we've been expecting you," said Mrs. Hill.

The blond girl on the floor stood and hung up the telephone. She introduced herself as Kerri Gold.

"Can one of you show Paige to her room?" asked Mrs. Hill. "She'll be rooming with Cassandra." She turned to me. "Dinner will be ready soon, but you have some time to freshen up."

"I'll show you where it is," said Kerri.

"Ah, but where is *my* roommate?" demanded Pia, crossing her arms and pouting again.

"I'm sure Katerina will be here shortly," said Mrs. Hill. "Be patient, Pia, and try not to overwhelm her when she gets here. Remember, Katerina's flying here all the way from Russia."

"Russia—that's some long trip, huh?" said Kerri, grabbing the bag Pia had carried and leading me down a hall. "Where are you from, Paige?"

"Nebraska," I said. "Wheeler, Nebraska."

"I'm from Laurel Beach, Florida," said Kerri. "What do you think of New York so far?"

"I don't know," I answered. "I mean, I haven't really seen that much of it."

"Yeah," said Kerri, "I know what you mean. I got in yesterday, and all I saw was the highway from the airport. Tomorrow they're supposed to take us on some kind of sight-seeing tour, though."

"That sounds like fun," I said.

"You're lucky to room with Cassandra," Kerri said. "She's really cool."

"Great," I said, trying to grin. The idea of a really cool roommate made me a bit nervous.

Kerri stopped in front of a closed door, knocked twice, and pushed it open.

"Cassandra, your roomie's here," she called over the dance music blaring out of a radio that was propped on the windowsill.

I looked around the room. There was a small window that looked out on the river, and twin beds with matching blue bedspreads were pushed up against opposite walls. There were also two small night tables and two wooden dressers. It was pretty clear which dresser was mine, because the top of the dresser on the far side of the room was piled with makeup and jewelry, and photographs were stuck around the frame of the mirror.

On the far bed sat a tall, slim girl with short black bobbed hair. She was busy painting her toenails red from one of the many bottles of polish on the night table. She had on a snug black jumpsuit that showed off her curvy figure, and a pair of big hoop earrings that shook as she nodded her head to the music. I had definitely never seen anyone in Wheeler in an outfit like that. In fact, she reminded me of the picture in the magazine that Kim had shown me back in my room when I was packing.

"Hey," she said, looking up at me with a quick smile.

"Hi," I said. "I'm Paige Sanders."

"Cassandra Contiago," she said, going back to applying polish to the big toe of her left foot.

Kerri turned the music down, then flopped onto the bed next to Cassandra.

"*Cuidado*—watch out!" exclaimed Cassandra. "You almost made me mess up!"

"Sorry," said Kerri. "You shouldn't be

doing that on the bed, anyway, you know. If Mrs. Hill catches you she'll be mad."

Cassandra shrugged. "I'm being careful." She looked at me. "You'll probably get to hear Mrs. Hill's list of rules later. 'Don't do this, don't do that,'" she singsonged, waving her polish brush in the air.

"Well, my mom can be pretty strict sometimes, too," I said. I sat down on the other bed. "So I'm used to it. It was even kind of hard to get my mom to agree to let me come to New York."

"Really?" said Cassandra, raising an eyebrow. "My mother's just the opposite. She's always let me do pretty much what I wanted."

Suddenly I felt embarrassed. I hoped Cassandra didn't think that what I had said sounded babyish.

"So, how did Ford find out about you, Paige?" asked Kerri.

"Actually, my grand…" I stopped. Now that would probably sound really hokey to them, I thought. I started again. "People have always told me I should model, so I sent them a picture," I said, adding a silent apology to my grandmother for my little white lie. "How about you guys?"

"Well, I did some modeling down in Florida," said Kerri. She stood up and stretched her arms up toward the ceiling, then she reached down toward her toes, bouncing in place. "Mostly catalog work and stuff for local stores—you know."

"Oh, sure," I said, although I didn't really.

"Anyway, a Ford scout spotted me on the beach and asked me to send them my pictures," said Kerri, standing upright again. "The next thing I knew they'd offered to take me on."

"Wow," I said. I couldn't help feeling a little jealous that Kerri had already been signed on by Ford. But then again, I thought, she already was a model when Ford found her. I, on the other hand, had no experience at all.

"I was discovered through the contest," said Cassandra. She finished the last of her toenails and capped the bottle of polish.

"The contest?" I repeated.

"Sure," said Kerri. "The Ford Supermodel of the World Contest. Pia was in it, too. And Naira—she's my roommate, you'll meet her."

"I guess you all do look kind of familiar," I said. I had watched the Supermodel of the World Contest on television just a few weeks

31

before with my grandmother. Nana had spent the entire two hours of the program telling me that I should have entered it. "What was it like, being in the contest?"

"Well," said Cassandra, "first I had to win the contest in my country, Brazil. Then I represented Brazil in the international contest."

"Wow," I said. "That must have been really exciting, being on television and everything."

Cassandra shrugged. "I'm used to being on television. In Brazil, I did a lot of commercials. I even had my own show."

"You're kidding," I said, amazed. "Your own *television* show?"

"Sure," said Cassandra. "It was called *Qual o lance?*—that means 'What's happening?' It was for teenagers. You know, all about the latest in fashion, what's in, celebrities. I have a tape of it, if you want to see it. But it probably wouldn't make much sense to you, since it's all in Portuguese."

"Portuguese?" I repeated, confused. "I thought you said you were from Brazil."

"I am," said Cassandra. She rolled her eyes. "Portuguese is what Brazilians speak."

"Oh, yeah," I said, blushing. "Right." How could I have made such a stupid mistake? I stood up quickly and bent over one of my suitcases, hoping Cassandra and Kerri wouldn't see how embarrassed I was. "Well, I guess maybe I'd better do some unpacking."

But when I unzipped my bag, the first thing I saw was Mr. Wigglesworth, my worn, stuffed rabbit. When I was really little, I'd slept with Mr. Wigglesworth every night. Now he was missing an eye and had several bald patches in his faded pink fur, but I'd always kept him on my bed anyway. I'd packed him at the last minute because I had thought he might help me feel less homesick. But there was no way I could unpack him now. Not after all the dumb things I had already said.

Luckily, Mrs. Hill called us in to dinner just then.

"Oh, well," I said, quickly zipping up my bag. "I'll just have to unpack later."

"That's what I like to hear," said Kerri, standing up. "Someone who's laid back about unpacking. My roommate, Naira, is organized beyond belief. She's been arranging her stuff since she got here this morning."

We made our way down the hall to the small dining area off the living room. Pia was setting the table and another tall, thin girl with smooth light brown skin and curly dark hair was sitting in one of the chairs. She was wearing a sleeveless red T-shirt and a pair of black pants. Her head was buried in one of those huge organizer date books.

"Speak of the devil," said Kerri. "I was just telling Paige here how incredibly organized you are, Naira."

Naira looked up from her book. She had amazing blue-green eyes.

"So what's your problem?" she asked. "I just like to know where all my things are."

Kerri grinned. "I'm just teasing, Naira. Actually, I wish I could get myself together to finish my own unpacking."

"Well, if you spent a little less time on the telephone with your friends back in Florida you'd be able to," said Mrs. Hill, walking into the room with a big bowl of pasta and vegetables. "Now, let's all eat."

"Nice to meet you, Paige," said Naira with a smile. She closed her date book and slipped it under her chair.

"It's nice to meet you, too," I said as I sat down.

"Ah, *che assurdo!* But this is ridiculous!" said Pia. She threw herself into a chair next to me. "This I cannot believe—we are now beginning dinner and still my roommate has not arrived!"

Just then the doorbell rang. Pia leaped up from her seat.

"I'll get it," said Mrs. Hill, giving her a stern look. "You all start eating before it gets cold."

Slowly Pia sat back down in her seat. Cassandra took a piece of chicken and passed me the platter.

Mrs. Hill opened the front door. A tall, thin girl with very pale skin and curly light brown hair walked in. She wore a simple black jumper with a white long-sleeved T-shirt underneath. Her curls were gathered into a high ponytail tied with a white chiffon scarf. What really struck me about her was the smooth, graceful way she moved. She seemed to float into the room, in spite of the fact that she was carrying a large brown leather suitcase which must have weighed a ton.

"Hello, dear," said Mrs. Hill. "You must be Katerina."

"*Da*—yes," said the girl softly. Her smile was so small and quick that I almost didn't see it. She put down her suitcase. "Hello."

"Well, you're just in time for dinner," said Mrs. Hill, waving toward the table. "If you'd like, I'll show you where to wash up first."

A few minutes later, Katerina came to the table. As she took her seat across from me, I couldn't help noticing how straight her back was. In fact, her posture was so good and she held her head so high on her long neck that she looked even taller than she was. She looked like she had had a lot of experience in modeling, unlike me. Even if I practiced for a million years I doubted if I could be that confident and calm.

"Hello, Katerina!" said Pia excitedly. "I am your roommate, Pia, from Italy."

"*Zdrazdvedje*—hello," said Katerina quietly, lowering her blue eyes to her plate.

"So," said Kerri, "you came all the way from Russia, right? That's a pretty long trip."

"Is this your first time in New York?" asked Naira.

"Yes," said Katerina. She lifted her chin slightly.

It was kind of weird, I thought, the way she just gazed out over everyone's heads, not really looking anyone in the eye.

"Well," said Mrs. Hill. "Now that you're all

here, it's a good time to discuss the house rules."

I heard Cassandra let out a small sigh next to me. Cassandra obviously wasn't into rules.

"First, and most important," said Mrs. Hill, "you must let me know where you are at all times. If you are planning to go to anything other than an event organized by Ford, I must be filled in on all the details. I need to meet whomever you will be with, and I will also need to know *exactly* what it is you will be doing and when I can expect you back."

Next to me Cassandra rolled her eyes. From what she had said about her mother, I knew that Mrs. Hill's rules must have sounded pretty childish to her, but to me, it was kind of reassuring. I had to admit, it was nice to know that someone actually cared where we'd be and what we'd be doing. I was used to telling my parents all that kind of stuff. In fact, it seemed pretty sensible—not that I was going to let anybody know that I thought so.

"Now," said Mrs. Hill, glancing at Kerri, "about the phone. I know that you'll all be anxious to talk to your families, and that's fine. But you must let me know when you are making a long-distance call. Also, please keep in mind that there is only one telephone line here for seven people, so try to keep your conversations brief, if possible.

"Finally, I expect you all to do your best to keep the apartment neat. That means putting your things away and making your beds in the mornings. And please, no food or drinks in the rooms. Are there any questions?"

"Yes," said Katerina, tilting her head gracefully. "I have a question."

"Yes?" asked Mrs. Hill.

"May I please be excused from dinner?" she asked. "I think I would like to go rest now."

"Of course, dear," said Mrs. Hill. "I imagine you must be tired. Let me show you to your room."

As she stood up and led Katerina down the hall, the table was silent for a moment.

"I think perhaps my roommate seems a little—how you say—*scontrosa,* unfriendly," said Pia, looking glumly down into her plate.

"She did seem kind of cold," said Cassandra.

"She hardly said anything," agreed Kerri.

"Oh, she's probably just really worn out

from her trip," said Naira. "She'll be bubblier tomorrow, you'll see."

"*Spero che si*—I hope so," said Pia, shaking her head.

I had to admit, I couldn't help feeling a little sorry for Pia. I wasn't really sure what to think of Katerina, but I could tell that Pia was pretty disappointed.

Later that night, I lay in my new bed, trying to fall asleep. There were so many unfamiliar sounds coming from outside and so much to think about that I just couldn't seem to relax. How can anyone sleep with all this noise, I thought, listening to the sounds outside on the street. At home, the only thing you could hear at night was the crickets.

But Cassandra seemed to be having no problem at all. I could hear her breathing deeply and evenly from her bed across the room from me.

I thought of my diary, tucked away in the suitcase under my bed. I always felt better when I wrote down how I was feeling. Maybe it would help me now.

Carefully, I leaned over and pulled my suitcase out from under my bed, unzipping it as quietly as I could. I reached inside and felt something soft and fuzzy—Mr. Wigglesworth. Groping around some more, I found the flowered-cloth-covered book and matching pen.

There had been no change in Cassandra's breathing at all, so I turned on the little light on my night table, hoping I wouldn't wake her. I didn't have anything to worry about. She didn't even budge.

I reached for my glasses on the night table, lay on my stomach, and opened my diary.

Well, here I am in New York, lying in bed listening to my roommate, Cassandra, sleep. I keep going over the meeting I had today with Eileen Ford, hoping I said and did the right things. I wonder how soon I'll know if they're going to offer to take me on as a Ford model— and what I'll say to them if they do! I really like the idea of being a model. But what if it turns out that I don't really have what it takes?

The other girls all seem so sure of themselves. A lot of them come from exotic places, and I think that everybody's had modeling experience except me.

But everyone has been pretty nice so far. Kerri's totally into fitness, which is probably why she has such a great body. Kerri and Cassandra already seem to be very good friends. It makes me feel a little left out. When I first got here, I said some really dumb stuff in front of Kerri and Cassandra. Now I bet they think I'm some kind of a country bumpkin or something.

Cassandra's exactly the way that I thought all models were. She looks like she's ready to have her picture taken at a moment's notice— she's always got makeup on and her wardrobe is unbelievable. I just hope that she's not disappointed in having me for a roommate.

Naira is from Chicago, so she's used to being in a big city like New York. She's also very organized. I bet she's gotten straight A's her whole life. I think she's sensible and down to earth, though. I'd like to be friends with her, but she's so independent that she doesn't seem to need anybody.

Pia's very cute and bubbly. She kind of reminds me of a puppy because she's so eager and excited about everything. Of course she's also so beautiful that if she were a puppy she'd be some fancy pedigree with an unpronounceable name. I don't think I'll tell her that she reminds me of a puppy though—she might be offended.

Speaking of offended, I don't know much about Katerina yet, but so far she's been pretty unfriendly and a bit weird. Of course, she's probably just tired from her trip. She does have incredible posture and walks very gracefully. I'll bet that she's done a lot of modeling to be able to move that way.

Writing this makes me think about how confident and experienced all the other girls are. How am I ever going to feel that sure of myself? I guess there's only one thing to do. I'll have to keep a close eye on everyone else in the next few days, and do my best to fit in. I'm in a new place, with new people, starting a new life—so now there's just going to have to be a new me!

CHAPTER 4

"Paige, will you take my picture?" asked Naira. "Try to get the Statue of Liberty in the background if you can. I'm organizing a scrapbook of New York for my little brothers back home, and I want to make sure I get all of the major sights in it."

"Sure," I said. I slid off the bench and took the camera she handed me. "Stand over by the railing."

It was the next afternoon, and the six of us were taking a trip around Manhattan on the Circle Line with Carla Harris. In the morning, Carla had picked us up at the apartment, and she'd been leading us around New York City since.

The day had started with my first ride on a New York City subway. Initially, it was terrifying. The train was very noisy, roaring through the underground tunnels and screeching as it rounded the corners. And it seemed as if it were going about a hundred miles an hour. But I held on tight to the metal pole and managed to keep my balance. I was really glad that Carla was there to tell us when to get off.

When we did get off, we were at the World Trade Center, the city's tallest skyscrapers. It turned out that we were having breakfast at this really fancy restaurant on the very top floor. It took ages just to get up to it on the elevator. Being up so high made me feel kind of queasy. Nobody else seemed to be bothered, so I forced myself to get over it by telling myself that the new me wasn't going to be afraid of heights. Then, before I knew it, I was used to being up there. By the time we'd finished eating, I was enjoying the view.

Next, Carla took us to South Street Seaport, where there was a big shopping center with a lot of fun stores and restaurants. And now we were on the Circle Line. Carla said it was a great way to see New York, since the boat traveled completely around the island of Manhattan.

Naira walked over to the side of the boat and leaned on the railing.

"Okay, say cheese," I said, snapping the picture just as the Statue of Liberty went by.

"Thanks," said Naira. She took a little notebook and a pen out of the black leather pack on her waist. "Statue of Liberty," she said to herself, making a check mark. I had always thought of myself as a fairly organized person, but compared to Naira I was a wreck.

"Excuse me, but *non capisco*, I do not understand," said Pia, as we slipped back into our seats. "Why did you ask that Naira say 'keys,' Paige?"

"No, not *keys, cheese*," I said, laughing a little.

"That's what you tell someone to say when you take their picture," explained Naira.

Pia looked confused. "Cheese? But why?"

"I don't know. I guess it's supposed to make them smile," I said, shrugging.

Pia leaned forward.

"Well, then, perhaps someone should ask my roommate to say 'cheese,'" she whispered. She nodded her head toward the other side of the boat.

I looked over and saw Cassandra and Kerri, who were busy talking. Behind them, Katerina was sitting by herself. As usual, Katerina held her head high and her back perfectly straight. She had the same reserved look on her face that she had had since she arrived, not smiling and not frowning, and she was gazing out over the water with her cool blue eyes. I sat up a little straighter myself. The new me was definitely going to have better posture.

"Whew, it's windy out here!" said Naira. She gathered her dark curls into one hand and tucked them under her red baseball cap.

"I know," I said, as the wind blew my own hair up around my face. "I'm going to be completely tangled tonight. My hair can be such a problem that way."

"But it is such a beautiful color," said Pia. She looked at Naira. "You both are so lucky to have such curls."

"Are you kidding?" said Naira. "The curls are what make it so unmanageable."

"Really," I agreed. Pia's long, thick, straight brown hair was pulled into a ponytail that nearly reached her waist. "Your hair is totally incredible, Pia. It's so smooth and shiny."

"Ah," said Pia, her blue eyes sparkling. "But that is thanks to my secret Italian recipe."

"Recipe?" asked Naira.

46

"That's right," said Pia. "You see, I rub some olive oil into it before I wash it."

"Olive oil?" I repeated. "You mean like in salad dressing?"

"*Certamente*, of course," said Pia. "But in Italy we use olive oil for much more than just salad. We cook with it and use it on pasta also. We even sometimes put it on our bread—like you Americans use butter."

Somehow, I couldn't imagine ever eating a piece of bread covered with oil, but I didn't say anything. The new me was through with making embarrassing comments.

"And it helps your hair, too?" asked Naira.

"Very much," said Pia, nodding. "If you put a little olive oil on the ends of your hair before you use the shampoo, when you are finished it is very—how you say—full of moisture, not so dried out."

"Wow," said Naira. "I'll have to try that."

Just then, Carla came over to our seats.

"I'm going inside to the snack bar," she said. "Does anyone want anything?"

I suddenly realized I was hungry. A cheeseburger and a soda would be great right now, I thought.

"Yes, please," said Pia. "I would like to have

a mineral water, if that is possible."

"I'm sure they have some kind of soda water," said Carla.

"They do," said Naira. "I was in there before. I'll take one, too, with lime. And one of those mini vegetable quiches."

Suddenly, the cheeseburger and soda I had been thinking of just didn't seem like the right thing for the new me to order.

"I'll have the same as Naira," I told Carla.

The rest of the boat trip was fun. We rode under a ton of bridges, and past the United Nations and the mayor's mansion. We went by Roosevelt Island, and I looked up and saw the red tram car dangling above the river. The new me will definitely get up the nerve to ride on that someday, I told myself.

After three hours, the boat tour was over, and Carla brought us all back to the apartment, where Mrs. Hill was making dinner.

"Time for some sit-ups," said Kerri. She lay down on the rug and hooked her feet under the edge of the couch.

"You must be kidding," said Naira, sitting in one of the white chairs near the window. "After a day like today? I'm beat."

"Me, too," I said, taking the other chair.

"Uck," said Cassandra, running her fingers through her short black hair. "I need to take a shower."

"Before you all go running off, I have some messages," said Mrs. Hill, reaching into the pocket of her apron and pulling out some slips of paper. "Kerri, call Jill Murray about scheduling a shoot. And your sister Casey and your friend Heather called from Florida."

"Excellent!" said Kerri. She jumped up and reached for the phone.

"Hold on just a minute," said Mrs. Hill sternly. "You're not the only one with phone calls to return."

Sheepishly, Kerri put the phone back.

"Katerina, your Aunt Sophia called from Brooklyn," said Mrs. Hill. "I didn't realize you had relatives in New York, dear."

"Thank you," said Katerina coolly. "I will call her back."

"Naira, Jill Murray wants you to call her about a possible booking," Mrs. Hill continued.

"Okay, thanks," said Naira.

"Oh, and Jill wanted me to tell Pia, Cassandra, and Paige that you're all scheduled for test photos with a photographer tomorrow morning," Mrs. Hill went on. "Remember to arrive at the shoot with clean hair and nails, and no makeup. Clothes will be provided by the stylist, as usual."

I felt my stomach do a little flip-flop.

"Did you say *me*, Mrs. Hill?" I asked.

"Why, yes, dear," Mrs. Hill replied. "The three of you are to report to Will Nichols's studio tomorrow morning at ten."

"Ah! Then I, too, must have a shower and wash my hair now," said Pia, heading toward the hall. "I'll use the second bathroom. Unless you wish to go first, Paige?"

"No, that's okay," I said. "I'll probably just have a bath later and then wash my hair to-morrow morning."

My mind was racing. I was scheduled for a session with a photographer the next day! I would have to get up early to wash my hair— it always turned out better if I let it air dry than if I blow-dried it.

What should I wear, I wondered. Even though they would have clothes at the studio for me, I wanted to look okay when I got there. Then I started to worry about the clothes they'd give me to wear. What if noth-ing fit right? Or worse, what if I looked terrible in everything they gave me?

And what had Mrs. Hill just said about makeup? That we weren't supposed to wear any to shoots? Did that mean that the pictures would be taken without makeup? Or maybe someone at the studio would put on our makeup for us—that must be it. The last time I'd let anyone do my hair and makeup, Kim had put my eyeliner on all crooked and piled my hair into a complete rat's nest. I'd looked like the bride of Frankenstein. Then I realized that whoever did my makeup would be a professional. But I still felt nervous thinking about it.

I was glad that Cassandra and Pia would be there too, since they had both had some experience with this kind of thing. I made up my mind to watch what they did.

Suddenly, I wanted to call home. I had so much to tell everyone, not only about my first day in New York, but that I'd been scheduled for my first session with a photographer, too.

"Mrs. Hill," I asked, walking into the kitchen. "Is it okay if I call Nebraska?"

"Why, certainly, dear," she said as she ran lettuce under the faucet. "Go ahead."

But it turned out that there was quite a

wait for the phone. Naira was already on it, talking to Ford, and when she finished, Kerri was on for ages. I looked for Katerina, remembering that Mrs. Hill had given her a message, too, but she wasn't around.

Actually, there was one good thing about waiting to use the phone. By the time it was my turn, everyone else had gone to their rooms to get ready for dinner, so I was be able to talk in private.

I looked at my watch as I dialed my family's number in Wheeler. Quarter to six. They should just be sitting down to dinner.

But the phone on the other end of the line rang and rang. That's weird, I thought. They always eat dinner at this time. Then I remembered—the time difference! It was two hours earlier in Nebraska, which meant it was only quarter to four.

I was about to hang up when my mother picked up the phone.

"Hello?" she said, a little breathlessly.

"Hi, Mom, it's me!" I said. I couldn't believe how happy it made me to hear her voice.

"Paige, honey! How are you? How's everything going?"

"Fine, Mom," I answered. "I'm having a

great time. We had a great tour of New York today, and tomorrow I'm testing with a photographer. Everybody's really nice here."

"Oh, that's great. Your father will be relieved to hear that you're doing well," said my mother. "He's been so worried about you. He'll be sorry he missed your call, though, honey. He took Danny and Erin into town to pick up some parts for the tractor."

"I didn't realize I was calling so early, Mom. I forgot the time difference," I explained. "It's just about dinnertime here."

"Oh, that's all right. It's just so good to hear your voice," she said. "I was out in the garden, getting some tomatoes for tonight's salad, and I thought I heard the phone. Of course, Nana was right here in front of the television in the den, but she's watching her program, so she's off in her own world."

I laughed. Every afternoon, from three to four o'clock, Nana watched her favorite soap opera. She'd been watching it for years, and she was completely involved in the characters' lives. For that one hour, nothing could make her budge. I doubted she had even noticed the phone ringing.

"Laura called," said my mother. "She was

wondering if we had any news from you, and she said to say hello. And Tommy stopped by."

"Oh?" I said, feeling that fluttery feeling in my stomach again.

"He didn't really say much," said my mother. "But I talked to Mrs. Nelson, and I have a feeling Tommy's wondering if you'll be back in time for the Teen Dance at the firehouse a week from Saturday. I told her we weren't sure yet, of course."

"Of course," I echoed. If Ford didn't offer to take me on, I'd probably be going home that day. If they did, who knew when I'd see Tommy again?

"Oh, here comes your grandmother. Her show must be over," said my mother. "Let me put her on to say a quick hello. You take care, sweetie, and we'll talk to you soon."

"Okay, Mom, bye," I said.

"Hello?" said my grandmother.

"Hi, Nana, how are you?"

"Oh, pretty good, considering," she said with a sigh.

"Considering what, Nana? Is something wrong?"

"Oh, no, not really," she said. "It's just that that sweet girl Gwen is going to go ahead and marry that nasty Farley. And everyone knows what an absolute cad he is."

It took me a moment to realize that she was talking about two of the characters on her soap opera.

"Oh, gee, Nana, that's too bad," I said. "Well, maybe it'll work out."

She snorted. "Are you kidding? Not a chance! But enough about my worries. How are *you* doing, Paige? Tell me, how's the life of a fashion model in the Big Apple?"

"Well, I'm not exactly a model *yet*, Nana," I said. "But I do have my first shoot with a photographer tomorrow."

"Oh, that's wonderful!" said my grandmother. "I just knew you'd be a big success out there, Paige."

"I hope so, Nana," I said. "But I've never really done anything like this before, you know."

"Oh, that's okay, Paige. Don't you worry about a thing; they'll love you," said my grandmother. "You just go ahead and be yourself."

"Uh, right, Nana," I said. That was the *last* thing I planned on doing.

CHAPTER 5

"Hi, come on in," chirped the woman who answered the door at Will Nichols's studio. She was very thin and had white blond hair pulled into a sleek bun at the nape of her neck. She reminded me a little of a canary except that she wore all black.

Pia, Cassandra, and I followed her inside. I had never seen anything like this place before. It was one gigantic room, with very high ceilings and huge windows along one wall. The floor was made of shiny light wood, kind of like the gym floors back at Wheeler High.

A long black table was covered with photographs, rolls of film, cameras, and other equipment. Against the windows was a taller metal table and several high stools. At the far end of the room, a huge roll of white paper was mounted on a wall. A few feet in front of the wall were several metal stands with lights and silver umbrellas attached to them. A blond man with a beard stood on a ladder adjusting one of the lights. He was dressed all in black, too. I wondered if it was some kind of uniform.

"I'm Stephanie, Will's assistant," said the skinny blond woman. "I'll be the stylist for today's shoot."

"Hello," said Pia.

"Nice to meet you," said Cassandra.

"Hi," I said. I wasn't sure what a stylist was, but it did sound familiar. Still, I knew it would be dumb to ask.

"Will!" Stephanie called out. "The models are here!"

"Wonderful!" said the bearded man, climbing down from the ladder. He walked toward us, wiping his hands on his jeans. "Hi, I'm Will Nichols. Okay, Stephanie, hair and makeup aren't here yet, so let's get them started with their clothes for now."

That's it, I remembered, a stylist has something to do with clothes. I looked down at my pink T-shirt and long gray cotton skirt and wondered again what I'd be wearing for the photographs.

Will Nichols paused and put his hands on his hips, looking at us.

"We usually have hair and makeup done first, but I'm on a very tight schedule today and I don't want to lose any time waiting. Let's see now—you're Pia, right? Yes, I saw your pictures from the Supermodel contest. I see her in something very simple, Stephanie, and let's keep the colors light, all right?"

"Okay, fine," said Stephanie.

"And you," he said, "you're Cassandra, yes? I've seen your contest photos, too—very nice. Stephanie, I want her in something very sophisticated and hip."

"Sure," said Stephanie.

He looked at me.

"And you must be Paige," he said. He turned to Stephanie. "Ford tells me that Paige is just starting to work on her book, so I'd like to try a couple of looks with her, if we have time. See what you can do to play up her hair color. Maybe something green. Or blue."

"All right," said Stephanie. "Why don't you come with me, girls?"

We followed her over to a large white folding screen. Behind the screen were several racks filled with clothing. There were tons of jeans, skirts, shirts, and dresses in a million different colors and styles. I couldn't help thinking of Kim and Laura back home, and of how much fun the three of us could have going through all this stuff.

"Let's see," said Stephanie. "Cassandra, why don't you try this on?" She handed Cassandra a black leather motorcycle jacket. "And I think maybe this miniskirt with this shirt."

"These are great," said Cassandra. She took the clothes from Stephanie and put the jacket on. She looked right at home in it.

"And Pia, put on these overalls with this shirt," said Stephanie, handing Pia some things. "By the way, I love your sweater. Where did you get it?"

I looked at Pia. Her sweater *was* amazing. It was oversized and looked like a knitted patchwork quilt—one arm was tan, the other green, the neck was brown and white, and the body was divided into two parts, green-and-brown stripes on one side and rust-colored with white flecks on the other.

"I made it myself," said Pia. She shrugged. "From some old sweaters I had. It was very easy."

I was impressed. The sweater looked like

something right out of a fashion magazine. I had been sure Pia was going to say she had bought it in some fancy boutique.

"What a great idea," said Stephanie. "How did you think of it?"

Pia shrugged. "*Non lo so*—I don't know, really. I make a lot of my clothes. I am very interested in fashion design."

"Well, you do seem to have a flair for it," said Stephanie. She turned to me. "Now, Paige honey, let me think, what should we put you in? Oh, I know—I have just the thing." She searched through the racks of clothes for a minute and handed me something stretchy and green. "Okay, girls, get dressed and come on out when you're ready."

We changed quickly behind the screen. Cassandra looked totally amazing in her leather jacket and miniskirt. She started doing poses right away. Pia's peach turtleneck with cream-colored polka dots and baggy faded overalls were really cute. The outfit matched her personality.

My outfit turned out to be a stretchy green sleeveless minidress. It was a good thing that I was having my hair and makeup done last. I couldn't imagine how I would have squeezed

60

into the dress without messing everything up. Don't get me wrong, I liked the dress a lot, but it was also much tighter and shorter than anything I'd ever worn before. I couldn't help feeling a little weird. No one I knew back in Wheeler ever wore stuff like this.

When we stepped out from behind the screen, Will Nichols was back on the ladder, and Stephanie was over by the metal table, talking to a man with a long brown ponytail and a woman with short, spiky black hair. They wore mostly black, too. Now I *really* wondered if it was a uniform. I was about to ask Cassandra, but as I opened my mouth I realized how mortified I'd be if I was wrong.

"Girls, this is Mario and this is Denise," said Stephanie, nodding for us to come over. "They're doing hair and makeup."

Denise smiled at us. Then she opened up a black case and started to arrange bottles, brushes, lipsticks, and other makeup items on the table.

"Well, Mario," said Stephanie. "What do you think about Pia?"

"Definitely," said Mario, nodding seriously. "I think it would be a very good move for her."

"That's how Will feels, too," said Stephanie. "I guess we should call Ford and see what they say." She looked at Pia. "Pia, how would you feel about a haircut?"

Pia's face grew pale.

"What did you say?" she stammered. "Cut my hair?"

"Will feels that a short cut would work better with the shape of your face," explained Stephanie.

"And I absolutely agree," said Mario. "For you a shorter cut would be much better."

"Mario could do it right here in the studio," said Stephanie. "His cuts are great. I'm sure you'll love it! And Will is never wrong about this sort of thing. What do you say we call Ford and see what they say?"

"*Si*, okay," said Pia quietly.

I couldn't help feeling sorry for Pia. All that beautiful hair! It must have taken forever for her to grow it so long.

"Great," said Stephanie, leading Pia away. "Mario, do you want to get started on Paige and Cassandra in the meantime?"

"All right," said Mario. He gathered up a bunch of my hair in his hands. "Let's see what we can do with this."

Suddenly I felt kind of nervous. What if they wanted to cut my hair, too? I didn't know if I'd be able to go through with it. I'd had long hair ever since I was little.

But to my relief, Mario ran his fingers through my hair and smiled. "Very nice," he said. "I think we'll do some hot rollers to add volume, and that's it. Have a seat."

I sat down on one of the high stools, being careful to pull down the hem of my minidress. Mario began to brush my hair. A few moments later I felt him pinning the hot rollers into place. I had never used rollers in my hair before, and I wondered how it would turn out.

"Now," said Mario, putting the last of the rollers in, "these need to sit for a couple of minutes. Meanwhile, Cassandra, why don't we see what we're going to do with you."

"Well, the woman who did my hair at the television station in Brazil used to roll it with a curling iron to give it height and then add a little mousse to hold it," said Cassandra, climbing up on the stool next to mine.

"You're from Brazil!" said Mario excitedly. "What part?"

"Rio," Cassandra answered.

"Oh, I adore Rio!" said Mario, brushing Cassandra's hair. "I've done a lot of work down there. Who did your hair in Rio?"

"Maria Silva," said Cassandra.

"Oh, sure, I know Maria—she's wonderful," said Mario. "We worked together on a movie that was filmed in the rainforest. I tell you, there's nothing as hard as trying to do hair in that kind of humidity!"

"A movie in the rainforest?" Cassandra repeated. "Was that *Tyler's Quest?*"

"Yes!" said Mario. "You saw it?"

"Actually," said Cassandra, "I interviewed the stars for my television program, *Qual o lance?*"

"How wonderful!" said Mario.

Great, I thought, feeling my scalp start to get warm—now Cassandra and Mario were practically best friends. Meanwhile it seemed like he had completely forgotten about me. I hoped my hair wasn't getting fried.

But to my relief, Mario was just about finished with Cassandra's hair.

"There," he said, arranging a couple of locks with his fingers. "You look great. Maria was absolutely right. Denise, you can start on her face if you want." He turned to me. "Ah,

Paige. Time to take your rollers out."

Just then, I saw Pia and Stephanie heading back over to us.

"Okay, Mario," said Stephanie. "Ford gave us the go-ahead. In fact, they think a short cut for Pia is an excellent idea."

"Wonderful!" said Mario. "Let me just finish up with Paige here, and we'll get started."

As Pia sat down on the other side of me, I looked at her, trying to figure out what she was thinking. But it was impossible to tell. She was kind of smiling, or at least her mouth was, but the rest of her face looked kind of funny.

Mario finished taking out my rollers and handed me the brush.

"Now, Paige," he said, "I'd like you to bend over and flip your hair upside down. Then give the underside of your hair a few strokes with the brush. This will give your hair a fuller look."

I stood up, bent over, and started brushing. When I was finished, I flipped my hair back into place. I could tell it was really puffing out a lot around my face. I hoped it didn't look too ridiculous.

"Perfect," said Mario, spritzing on some

hair spray. "Now, Pia, let's get started."

"Okay, Paige," said Denise. "You're next for makeup." She finished brushing some deep red lipstick onto Cassandra's lips.

I looked at Cassandra's face. You could tell she was pretty made-up, but she looked great. Her skin looked completely smooth, and Denise had put some dark eyeliner around her eyes, which really made them stand out.

"Okay, Cassandra, Will's ready to start with you," said Stephanie. I watched Cassandra strut over to the far end of the room. I couldn't believe how confident she was.

"All right," said Denise, leaning toward me. She took off my glasses and put them on the table behind me. I closed my eyes and felt her spreading liquid makeup on my face with a little sponge. It felt wet and thick. I wondered how much she was putting on.

Denise continued to make me up, putting on what felt like tons of eye shadow, eyeliner, mascara, and eyebrow pencil. It was hard to keep from blinking with her doing all that stuff to my eyes.

Meanwhile, I could hear the snip of Mario's scissors to my right. I wondered what Pia's hair looked like, and how she was taking it. I tried to sneak a peek between coats of mascara, but without my glasses everything was a blur.

Finally, Denise was finished with my make-up. I turned to reach for my glasses on the table.

"Oh, no, don't put those on," said Denise.

"But I can't see without them," I told her.

"Well, they're going to smudge your face," said Denise. "Besides, I'm sure Will won't want to photograph you in them."

And *I'm* sure I won't even be able to *find* Will without them, I thought. But I supposed it made sense. After all, you didn't see too many pictures of models in glasses. But how was I going to see my way across the room without them? Then I had an idea. I picked up my glasses and turned them backward, so the earpieces stuck out away from me. Holding them a couple of inches from my eyes, I could peer through them without ruining my makeup.

I looked over at Pia and was shocked by what I saw. She was still sitting with that same stiff little smile on her face, and her hair was incredibly short. It was shorter even than Cassandra's. In fact, it almost looked like it could be a boy's haircut. The amazing thing was, it did look really good on her. But I couldn't help thinking, as I looked at the piles of long, thick, brown hair on the floor around her, that if it had been me I would have been in tears.

"Oh, good, Paige, you're finished," said Stephanie, walking over. "Will's just about ready for you. Pia, you look marvelous, darling!"

Holding my glasses backward in front of my face with one hand and yanking down the hem of my miniskirt with the other, I made my way over toward the other side of the room. The roll of white paper had been pulled down to cover the wall and part of the floor, and Cassandra was standing on it, leaning on one hip, running one hand through her hair.

"Fabulous!" Will Nichols was saying as he moved around her with his camera. "You look great! Now tilt your head a little to the left. Beautiful, Cassandra! Now smile, laugh. Okay, a little more serious now."

As I watched Cassandra moving easily from pose to pose with the lights flashing around her, I began to get kind of nervous. I could tell she knew exactly what to do. I hoped Will Nichols wouldn't be disappointed with me.

"Okay, Cassandra, that was great," said Will. "I think we got some really good shots. Paige, let me just change rolls and I'll be right with you."

"Phew," said Cassandra, taking off her leather jacket. "This jacket is hot." Her face lit up. "*Puxa*—wow! Pia! You look amazing!"

I turned my head, held my glasses up to my eyes, and saw Pia walking toward us, her face made-up and the wispy bangs of her new short hair fluffed over her forehead.

"Really," I agreed. "You look great."

"Fantastic," said Will, walking over to us. "Mario did an excellent job."

"Thanks," said Pia, smiling. "I think I will like it, too."

"I'm sure this new look will get you a lot of work," said Will. "Now, why don't you just sit down and relax while I start with Paige."

As I watched Pia take a seat nearby, I couldn't help wishing she would go wait somewhere else. I mean, Pia was nice and everything, but I already felt pretty self-conscious about my first photo shoot. I knew that having her watch wasn't going to make me feel much better. Then, to my surprise, Cassandra pulled up a chair next to her and sat down, too. Great, I thought—now they're both going to see that I have no idea what I'm doing.

"Okay, Paige," said Will, snapping shut his camera. "Let's see what you've got."

I put my glasses down on an empty chair. Everything was blurry, but I wasn't about to embarrass myself by groping my way around, so I took a deep breath, pulled down the hem of my dress, and tried to walk confidently in the direction of the white paper.

The next thing I knew, I felt something brush my arm. Then there was a big crashing sound. A metal pole slammed onto the ground in front of me, and a silver umbrella bounced by. I could see them, that's how close they were to me.

"Oh my gosh, did I do that?" I said. "I'm so sorry!"

"That's all right, no problem at all," said Will, reaching for the pole. "I'm just glad it didn't hit you. Give me a moment and I'll have it back up."

I could feel my face getting redder by the

second as Will pulled over the ladder, climbed it, and reattached the umbrella to the pole. How could I have done something so stupid? I looked over at Cassandra and Pia, wondering if they were laughing at me. But without my glasses, their faces were too blurry for me to tell.

Finally, Will was ready. I walked onto the white paper and looked at the camera. I had absolutely no idea what to do.

"Okay, now, Paige," said Will, starting to snap photos. "Just try to loosen up. Relax your arms a little, not so stiff."

As the lights flashed around me, I shook my arms, trying to get them to relax. But I couldn't figure out where to put them. They felt clunky just hanging by my sides, so I tried putting them on my hips, but that made my dress ride up. I tried to smile as I yanked it back down. Finally, I just crossed my arms over my chest.

Will Nichols moved the camera away from his face. I couldn't tell what was going on because I couldn't see his expression.

"I've got an idea," he said. "Maybe a little music would help. Stephanie! Put something fun on the stereo, would you?"

I sighed. I could tell I was doing pretty badly, and I'd only just started. After all, Cassandra hadn't needed any music. I just knew that Will Nichols must be disappointed.

But a few moments later, the two stereo speakers behind Will Nichols began blaring some upbeat rock music. I had to admit that it did help. Somehow, it was much easier to relax with the music playing. I swung my arms to the beat and took a couple of steps.

"That's it, that's better," said Will Nichols, snapping away with his camera. "Now give me a little smile, Paige, not so serious. Try to look like you're having fun."

I did my best to relax for the next few minutes. Acting like you're having fun isn't as easy as it sounds, though, especially when you feel like your stomach is tied up in one big knot.

Finally, Will Nichols put down his camera.

"Stephanie!" he called. "I'd like to try Paige in something else, something with a more casual look. Paige, why don't you go on over to Stephanie so she can change your outfit? Pia, let's get started on you."

I sighed. I knew the tight green dress wasn't really right for me. I just couldn't seem to get comfortable in it.

I made my way very slowly and carefully toward the edge of the white paper. As I passed Pia, she handed me my glasses.

"Here," she whispered. "*Attenzione*—careful."

"Thanks," I answered, embarrassed. I took the glasses from her and held them in front of my face.

As I walked back toward Stephanie and the white screen I could hear Will directing Pia.

"Beautiful!" he said. "Fantastic! Now lift your chin a little higher—great!"

I sighed. It was pretty obvious just from what Will Nichols was saying that Pia was doing a much better job than I had.

But the next outfit Stephanie gave me to wear made me feel better. The big denim shirt tied at the waist and the cut-off shorts, although shorter than I was used to, were much more like the things I wore at home, on the farm. I felt pretty normal and relaxed in these clothes, especially compared to how I'd felt in that tight minidress.

I walked back toward the others and sat down in the chair next to Cassandra. Pia was posing for the camera, and of course, she was really good at it. She moved easily in front of

Will, turning her head from side to side, smiling, throwing her arms out, and kicking her feet out. As far as I could tell, she wasn't nervous at all. Her bubbly personality definitely showed in every move she made. She was just as good as Cassandra, but in a different way.

When Pia was done, Will called me back out in front of the camera. I put my glasses back down on the chair and carefully walked out onto the white paper.

I took a deep breath and turned to face the camera. This time, I was determined to relax. The music helped, and so did the clothes, but I still couldn't help wishing I was better at this modeling stuff. Cassandra and Pia had both made it look so easy.

After a little while, Will put down his camera again.

"Paige, I'd like you to try something," he said. "I want you to imagine that you're somewhere else."

"Excuse me?" I said, squinting in the direction of his voice.

"Think of someplace that makes you feel comfortable," he said. "Someplace that always makes you feel happy."

Suddenly, an image of the pond behind

74

our farm popped into my head. The pond was one of my favorite places in the whole world. Our family and the Nelsons used it for swimming in the summer and skating in the winter. And on warm spring days, I would go there by myself to write in my diary.

"Great," said Will, starting to snap his camera. "Now I want you to keep the image of that place in your mind. Don't just think about it—try to actually feel like you're there."

I took a deep breath. I imagined that I could smell the cornflowers and Indian paintbrush that grew in the field nearby and hear the quacking of the ducks that came back to the pond every spring. I was hardly aware of the lights flashing and Will moving around me with his camera. I just kept thinking about the pond. I remembered skipping stones there with my brother and sister, and my father teaching me to swim there when I was little. I thought of the time when Tommy and I were kids. He had boasted that he could balance on a log in the water, then ended up falling in with all his clothes on. The image of an eight-year-old Tommy, completely drenched with a surprised look on his face, came to my mind, and suddenly I burst out laughing.

"Oh, sorry," I said to Will, putting my hand up to my mouth.

"No, no, that was great," he said. "Really great, Paige. I think I got some good shots, especially toward the end there. Nice work. You can sit down now."

I made my way carefully past the lights and umbrellas and over to where Pia and Cassandra were sitting.

"You were very good at the end of this shoot," Pia told me.

"Yeah," said Cassandra. "You should get some good shots from this."

"Thanks," I said, feeling pleased.

But the next moment, I was exhausted. This whole thing had been harder than I had expected. Then I realized that it had gotten kind of fun in the end—especially the part where Will had made me think about the pond. It had helped me feel a lot more relaxed than when we'd started out, and maybe that meant I had done okay after all. I only hoped that some of the pictures would turn out well enough for Ford to use them in my book.

"Okay, everyone," said Will Nichols. "That about wraps it up. You all did very well. I'll send the photos over to Ford when they're ready."

Tired, I decided to sit down and relax for a minute before I went to change. But as I flopped down on the nearest chair, I felt something underneath me and heard a loud crack. Then I realized what had happened.

CHAPTER 6

"Can you see out of those things?" Cassandra asked me, as the three of us made our way up the last block toward home.

"Yeah, I'm fine," I said. I put my hand up to feel the black electrical tape Stephanie had given me to hold my broken earpiece onto my glasses. "I just can't believe I did that."

"You should probably get contacts anyway," said Cassandra. "That way you don't have to wear your glasses to photo shoots at all."

"*Si*, absolutely," said Pia, shaking her new bangs off her face. "You should get contact lenses, Paige. You have such beautiful eyes, you shouldn't hide them behind those glasses all the time."

"It would definitely be a more sophisticated look," said Cassandra. "Especially now that your glasses are fixed with tape."

I thought about it. My glasses had always seemed fine to me, but now maybe contacts did make sense. They *would* make things a lot easier at photo shoots. And, like Cassandra had said, I'd seem more sophisticated without my glasses. It could be like a new look to go with the new me.

"Maybe you guys are right," I said. "Maybe it's a good idea."

"*Certo,* of course it is," said Pia. "And now I have another good idea. Let's all go have a coffee."

"Great idea," said Cassandra, "that's just what I need."

"Yesterday, when we were coming back from the sight-seeing with Carla, I saw a coffee bar near here that looked *molto bello*— very nice," Pia said.

"Gee, shouldn't we call Mrs. Hill and let her know where we're going?" I asked.

Cassandra sighed.

"No, no, Paige is correct," said Pia. "Come, we must call Mrs. Hill first."

We found a phone booth nearby and made the call. Then we walked a couple of blocks to the coffee bar, talking and laughing. I'd never been to a coffee bar before, so I wasn't sure what to expect. It turned out that it was just like a little cafe. There was a big green marble counter with stools at one end, and small, matching round green tables all over. Gold script on the big plate-glass window said THE COCOA BEAN.

"This is so cute," I said, as we sat down at one of the tables.

"And *molto autentico*—very authentic," said Pia. "In Italy, there are coffee bars like this everywhere." She picked up the little plastic menu cards that were wedged between the sugar dispenser and the bottle of flowers on the table and handed us each one. She looked completely at home.

"Oh, look," said Cassandra, studying the little card. "They have *cafezinho!*" She looked at us happily. "That's a special coffee from Brazil."

I looked down at the menu, wondering what I should order. They seemed to have every kind of coffee in the world here. Too bad I had never really liked coffee. My parents drank it every morning, but it had always tasted bitter to me. There was hot chocolate on the menu, but hot chocolate seemed more like a winter drink. Besides, I thought, wouldn't ordering hot chocolate seem kind of babyish and unsophisticated?

Just then, I heard a deep voice above me.

"May I take your order?"

I looked up and straight into a pair of the greenest eyes I had ever seen. The guy they belonged to had wavy dark brown hair, and he was smiling directly down at me, a pad and pen in his hand. He was definitely one of the cutest guys I had ever seen. For a moment I couldn't say anything.

"Well, I'm ready," said Cassandra, gazing up at the waiter. "I'd like a *cafezinho*."

"And I would like to have an espresso, please," said Pia.

The waiter looked back at me and smiled again, his green eyes sparkling.

"Uh—I'm not sure," I stammered. I fumbled with my menu. Just pick something, I told myself, anything. Stop acting so silly.

"Do you mind if I suggest something?" he asked.

"Uh, no," I said, looking back up at him. "I mean, sure, that would be nice."

"Well, the iced choco-cappuccino is pretty good," he said, leaning over to point it out on my menu.

"Sure, that sounds fine," I said, feeling my cheeks redden.

"Okay," he said. He scribbled on his pad, then nodded at us. "Be right back."

"Well, I'd say someone was awfully impressed with *you*, Paige," said Cassandra as the waiter walked away.

"*Sicuramente!*" said Pia. "That boy was definitely—how you say—very interested."

"In *me?*" I said. I blushed again. "No way."

"Oh, come on, Paige," said Cassandra. "It was completely obvious. He hardly looked at me at all. His eyes were glued to you the whole time he was at our table."

"And I would say that your eyes, also, were doing some gluing to him from behind those glasses," said Pia. She wiggled her eyebrows at me mischievously.

Oh my gosh, I thought, my glasses! I had completely forgotten about the black tape holding them together. The guy must have thought I looked ridiculous.

"If he was staring at me, it's because I look so silly with this tape on my glasses," I said.

Cassandra grinned. "Believe me, Paige, he wasn't looking at your glasses."

"He was just taking our order, that was all," I protested. But I was beginning to wonder—*had* something special gone on between us in those few moments?

Just then, he came back with our drinks on a tray. Pia and Cassandra both had these great big grins on their faces. I had to look straight down at the table to keep from laughing.

After putting Pia's and Cassandra's cups on the table, he placed a tall, frosted glass in front of me.

"I also brought you some whipped cream and cinnamon," he said, putting two small bowls down near my chocolaty drink.

"Thanks," I murmured. I stared down at the table; I didn't want to blush *again*.

"Sure, no problem," he said. "Hope you like it."

"No problem," teased Cassandra in a low voice as he walked away. "Hope you like it."

"I brought you some cream and cinnamon," mimicked Pia, giggling.

"Oh, come on, you guys," I protested. "You're making a big thing out of nothing."

"What's the matter, Paige?" asked Cassandra. "Don't you think he's cute?"

"Well, sure, but .."

"Paige probably has a boyfriend back home," said Pia. "Am I right?"

They both looked at me.

"Well, not really," I said. I concentrated on putting a spoonful of whipped cream into my glass. "I mean, there is this guy, but I guess you couldn't really call him a boyfriend."

"You and this 'guy'—have you made any promises to each other?" asked Pia.

"No," I said, shaking my head. Not only had Tommy and I not made any promises, we hadn't even ever talked about what went on between us that last night.

"Then, there's no problem," said Cassandra. "You're completely in the clear to go for this guy."

"Aren't you forgetting something, Cassandra?" I asked. "This guy and I don't know each other at all. I mean, we hardly even spoke to each other."

Cassandra waved her hand as if she were shooing away a fly.

"Don't worry," she said. "He likes you. You like him. What else do you need?"

"I don't know," I said, shrugging. After all, Cassandra clearly had a lot more experience with guys than I did. One kiss in back of a barn didn't exactly make me an expert.

I took a sip of my iced choco-cappuccino. To my surprise, it was actually good. It had a yummy chocolaty taste, almost like a chocolate soda. Mixed with the whipped cream and the cinnamon, it was delicious. I could hardly even taste the coffee at all. Before I knew it, I had finished the whole thing.

Pia and Cassandra had finished their drinks, too.

"Now," said Cassandra, "where is that waiter of yours, Paige?"

"I see him," said Pia, waving across the room at him. "Check, please."

As the waiter came over I suddenly got that same fluttery feeling inside that I had felt when I was near Tommy. This is silly, I told myself. I don't even know this guy. But there was something about him that made me feel like I *did* know him.

"Here you go," he said, smiling at me and putting our check facedown on the table. "Thanks a lot."

"Wow!" said Cassandra when he walked away. "What did I tell you? He's totally smitten."

Pia nodded. "He is, how you say, heels over head for you, Paige."

I shook my head and laughed. "You mean 'head over heels,' Pia, and I still think this is all in your minds. Look, he probably treats all his customers that way. He's just a nice guy."

"Oh, yeah?" said Cassandra, turning over the check. "Then how do you explain *this*?"

I looked down at the little green paper in her hand. There, written in blue ink, were the words:

It's on me. Hope you liked the
choco-cappuccino. Come back soon.
                                        Jordan

CHAPTER 7

I've been in New York for a total of five days. So far I've been to three test photo shoots. Yesterday I went to one shoot in the morning, and one in the afternoon. Amazingly enough, I'm starting to get used to it all, both the modeling and the city. The more Carla shows us around, and the more I learn about the city, the more at home I feel. In a way, Wheeler and the farm seem far away now. Well, I guess they really are far away.

It's morning, and everyone else went to a museum with Carla, but I'm supposed to meet with Jill Murray at Ford in a little while, so I didn't go. Jill wants me to come over and take a look at the pictures from my first test shoot, the one with Will Nichols. I'm so excited to see them—I hope some of them turned out okay.

Mom called last night after dinner, which was great, because I finally got to talk to the whole family. Nana asked me all about the shoot and, as usual, gave me the latest on her soap opera. Erin told me all about her new school clothes. Of course, all Danny wanted to know was if I was coming back or if he could have my room! Brothers!

It made me feel a little sad to talk to Dad, because I could hear in his voice how worried he still was. I guess part of it is that he's never been to New York, so he thinks of it as this really scary place. If only he had some kind of crystal ball or something so he could see what things are like here (how nice all my housemates are, and how well Carla and Mrs. Hill take care of us), I know he'd feel better.

After I had talked to everyone, Mom got back on the phone. She told me that Scooter wanders around the house all day meowing and looking for me. He also sleeps on my bed at night, which made me really miss him. She also told me something kind of funny about Tommy. It turns out that after my mother told Mrs. Nelson that she didn't know if I would be home in time for the Teen Dance, Tommy asked Kim to go with him. I guess that's okay. I mean, like Pia and Cassandra were saying, it's not like we made any promises to each other, so I guess *we're both free to go out with anyone we want. It does make me feel a little weird, though, to think of Tommy going to a dance with one of my best friends.*

If only I'd gotten a chance to talk to that guy Jordan at the Cocoa Bean the other day. He was so cute. Pia and Cassandra were totally convinced that he liked me. But it's kind of hard to get to know someone when they're just taking your order and bringing you coffee. I wonder how old he is. He looks about my age or maybe a little older. Maybe I can get Pia and Cassandra to go back there with me sometime. I wonder how often he works.

I closed my diary, capped my pen, and put them back next to Mr. Wigglesworth in the suitcase under my bed. It was time to get ready to go to Ford.

I walked over to the closet I shared with Cassandra. There was a huge difference between our clothes. My clothes were practically every color of the rainbow; most of Cassandra's were black. My jeans, sweaters, and shirts looked so average next to Cassandra's elegant and "hip" wardrobe. I touched the black jumpsuit she had worn on the day I met

89

her. Now *that* would be a cool thing to wear to my meeting with Jill. But I couldn't take something of Cassandra's without asking. I would just have to make do with what I had.

I finally settled on a green and white checked sleeveless, button-down shirt and my black jeans. After all, Will Nichols had said something about green bringing out the color of my hair, right? Now, if only I'd had a chance to get my glasses fixed. I had replaced the black electrical tape with some clear tape that Mrs. Hill had given me, but you could still see where they were broken. I wished I could just go without them, but that was definitely out of the question. I couldn't even take them off once I got to Ford, or I'd never be able to see my own pictures.

I walked out into the living room. I was surprised to find Katerina there, dressed in a purple leotard and black tights, sitting in the middle of the floor. Her legs were stretched out straight in front of her, toes pointed. She was leaning forward over them, her stomach touching the tops of her thighs and her chin resting on her knees.

"Wow," I said. "You are so flexible!"

She looked up at me in surprise.

"Oh," she said, scrambling to her feet. "I didn't know anyone else was here."

"Me, neither," I said. "I thought you'd gone to the museum with the others."

She shook her head. "I requested to stay here."

"Well, don't stop because of me," I said. "Actually, I was just leaving. I can't believe how limber you are, though. Do you dance or something?"

"Yes," she said, lifting her chin slightly. "I mean, I used to. I studied ballet in Russia. Now I just practice on my own."

"Wow, that's great!" I said. "I bet it really helps your modeling, too."

"Yes, I suppose," she said. She turned away and headed toward her bedroom.

"Hey," I called after her, "like I said, don't stop on my account, Katerina. I'm leaving now anyway."

But she was already down the hall. The next thing I heard was the sound of her bedroom door closing.

I shook my head. Katerina definitely wasn't one of the friendliest people I had ever met.

An hour and a half later I pulled open the

door to the red brick townhouse of Ford Models. I walked inside and went up to the second floor to find Jill Murray.

She looked up from some papers on her desk with a smile. "Hi, Paige," she said. "Nice to see you. Have a seat."

"Hi," I said. I sat down in the chair across from her.

"Well, let's look at the pictures from your test with Will Nichols." She picked up a large manila envelope on her desk. "It looks as though we got some nice shots." She opened the envelope, pulled out several plastic sheets filled with slides, and handed them to me. "See what you think."

I scanned the top row of slides on the first sheet. I could tell that these were from the beginning of the shoot. My body looked kind of stiff, and I was looking down instead of into the camera. It was as if my thoughts actually showed up in the pictures. I looked scared, nervous, and unhappy. How could I not have realized what an unhappy look I had on my face? In a couple of the slides, I was even frowning. No wonder Will had kept telling me to smile. Just looking at the pictures made me feel a bit uncomfortable again.

But it was amazing what a difference the professional hairstyling and makeup made. In some of the pictures, I hardly even recognized myself. My hair looked thick and soft, and the makeup made my eyes stand out. It was definitely kind of cool to see what I looked like without my glasses, too.

The slides got better and better as I worked my way down the sheet and onto the next one. In a few of them, I actually looked like I was happy. And there was one that Will must have snapped without my realizing it. In it, I was kind of staring off into the distance, as if I were daydreaming.

The best pictures of all were the ones at the end, when I had been wearing the denim shirt and shorts and Will had told me to think about the pond. Even the one where I had burst out laughing was kind of cute.

"I think on the whole they turned out very nicely, Paige," said Jill. "I know your first shoot can be tough. But I think we've got a couple here that we can use for your book."

"Really?" I asked. I hoped she wasn't just being nice.

"Sure," she answered. "I think these, in particular, would work quite well." She pointed to the daydreaming one and the one where I was laughing. "Several of the shots show off your features, but these two seem the most natural."

I nodded. "I see what you mean."

"Good, then it's settled," said Jill. "We've got the first two pictures for your book."

"Great," I said, with a huge smile.

"And the pictures from yesterday's shoots should be in sometime today," Jill went on. "Once I have a chance to look at them, I'll give you a call. I'm sure we'll have more pictures for your book."

"I hope so," I said.

"Now, tell me," said Jill, "how are you doing otherwise? How's everything going for you in New York?"

"Fine," I said. "I really like it here."

"Well, please don't hesitate to let me know if there's anything at all I can help you with," she said. "Any questions or problems that might arise."

"Actually, there *is* something you can help me with," I said, playing with the tape on my glasses. "I need to know where I should go to get contact lenses."

"No problem," said Jill. "There's a great

place not too far from your apartment that does glasses and contacts. Here, let me just write down the address for you."

She handed me a slip of paper.

"Thanks," I said, taking the paper from her and standing up.

As I made my way down the stairs of the Ford townhouse to the first floor, I felt a shiver of excitement run through me. The pictures had turned out okay, and I was starting to fill up my book. For the first time since I'd arrived in New York, I actually felt like I had a chance at being a real professional model!

Later that afternoon I walked out of Eye Spy, the store that Jill had sent me to. My new contacts were in, and it was strange to look around without seeing the edges of my glasses. My eyes felt kind of funny, and I wanted to blink a lot, but the optometrist who had fitted me for the lenses had said that eventually I would get used to them.

She had also convinced me to get my glasses repaired. At first I didn't really see why, since I would probably be wearing my contacts from now on. But the optometrist explained that it's always a good idea to have a pair of glasses as a backup, so I agreed.

The amazing thing was how little time it had all taken. Back in Wheeler, whenever I got a new pair of glasses I had to wait two weeks for them to be ready. The woman at Eye Spy had done an eye exam to test my prescription, given me the contacts, and fixed my glasses all right while I was there in the store.

But I was starting to realize that a lot of things in New York were like that. You could wait while your shoes were fixed, your film was developed in an hour, and you could walk in off the street for a haircut or a manicure. I guessed it was really important to New Yorkers to be able to get anything they wanted done whenever they wanted it.

Just the other day, I had seen a menu for a Chinese restaurant that delivered twenty-four hours a day! It was hard to imagine having anything like that back in Wheeler. But then again, it was also hard to imagine many people in Wheeler who would want to order egg rolls at three o'clock in the morning.

I had a thought as I walked back toward the apartment. Maybe I should pass by the Cocoa Bean on my way home. After all, it was only a block or so out of my way. Not that I actually had the guts to go inside or anything, but maybe if Jordan were working I could manage to sneak another look at him through the window.

As I turned the next corner and headed up the block toward the Cocoa Bean, I could feel my heart beating faster. I knew it was crazy—after all, I hardly knew Jordan—but there was something about the idea of seeing him again that made me feel really good.

The closer I got to the Cocoa Bean, the more nervous I felt. It was funny, but in a way my face felt kind of naked without my glasses. I had never realized how safe I'd always felt looking at the world from behind them. What if Jordan saw me peering through the window? Would he know I was looking for him? I'd better make sure to peek in very casually, so it wouldn't look like I was staring.

I took a deep breath. I would pass the front of the Cocoa Bean in just a moment. I swung my arms and did my best to look relaxed. Turning my head ever so slightly to the left, I peered out of the corner of my eye.

To my surprise, Jordan was right at the big plate-glass window, polishing it with a cloth. I had expected to have to peer into the back of the room to see him. I was so shocked to see him so close that I stopped in my tracks and my mouth dropped open.

As soon as he saw me he smiled and waved. Before I even knew what I was doing, I waved back. Jordan signaled me to wait a moment and put down his cloth. I tried to stay calm as I watched him make his way through the maze of little round tables and out onto the street.

"Hi," he said, grinning. "You came back."

"Hi," I said. "Actually, um, well, I was just passing by."

He frowned suddenly. "You look kind of— *different*, somehow."

"Oh, it must be…" I started, but I stopped myself. No need to remind Jordan about the silly-looking, taped-up glasses I had been wearing when he met me. "I don't know," I said. I looked down.

"Well, *something's* different," he said. He shook his head and frowned. Then he shrugged. "Hey, want to come in and have something to drink?"

"I can't, really," I said. It was getting kind of close to dinnertime. Mrs. Hill would be expecting me.

"Didn't you like your delicious iced choco-cappuccino?" he asked.

"Oh, sure," I said. "It was great. It hardly even tasted like coff..." I stopped. "I mean, it was one of the best coffees I've ever had."

"Yeah, it's not too bad," said Jordan. "For coffee."

"Don't you like coffee?" I asked, surprised.

He grinned. "I bet you thought I was a big coffee drinker because I work here, right?"

I nodded sheepishly.

"That's okay," he teased. "I never really liked the taste. That's why I go for the choco-cappuccino. The chocolate kind of covers up the coffee flavor."

"It almost tasted like a chocolate soda," I said. "By the way, thanks for paying our check. That was really nice."

"Sure," said Jordan. He paused. "Listen, um, maybe we can go out somewhere together sometime." He laughed. "Someplace where *someone else* can be the waiter and we can really talk."

"That would be great," I said. I could feel my heart beating faster.

"How about lunch tomorrow?" he asked. "I know a nice place that's close by."

"Okay," I said. Then I thought of something. "Maybe you should pick me up so I can introduce you to Mrs. Hill. She's sort of like a chaperone for me and my housemates."

"No problem," he said. "Just tell me where I'm supposed to go."

He dug into the back pocket of his jeans and handed me a pen and a small pad. I wrote down the address and phone number of the apartment.

"Great," he said, taking back the pad. "I'll come get you at one o'clock, okay?"

"Okay, Jordan," I said, starting down the street. "See you then."

"Hold on a minute!" he called after me.

I turned.

"This is kind of embarrassing, but I realized I don't even know your name!"

"Paige!" I called back happily. "Paige Sanders!"

But the truth was I didn't feel like Paige Sanders at all. Walking down a New York City street, wearing my new contact lenses, and knowing I was about to have the first real date of my life, I felt like I was finally the new me!

CHAPTER 8

Back at the apartment, I found Kerri, dressed in cut-offs and a red T-shirt that said LAUREL HIGH PEP SQUAD, sitting on the edge of Cassandra's bed doing arm curls with a small yellow dumbbell. Cassandra stood in the middle of the room in a short white satin bathrobe, holding two dresses up in front of her.

"Which one?" asked Cassandra.

"Definitely the red," said Kerri. She raised the dumbbell to her shoulder while breathing in evenly. "I mean, the black's nice too, but the red one will really get you noticed. Don't you think so, Paige?"

I looked at the two dresses. I kind of preferred the black one, which was long and simple. But anyone who wore the red one, with its scooped back and short, flouncy skirt, would get a lot of attention—even I could see that. And, of course, it would look great on Cassandra.

"Yeah, I guess the red one's more exciting," I said, flopping down on my bed.

"Good, then it's settled," said Cassandra. She hung the black dress back up in the closet and took the red one off its hanger.

"Where are you going?" I asked.

"Oh, I'm supposed to go out to dinner with Jill Murray and Milo Manning," said Cassandra.

"Milo Manning," I said. "Why does that sound familiar?"

"Probably because he's one of *the* hottest designers in the country," said Kerri. She switched the dumbbell to the other hand.

"Oh," I said. "Sure, of course."

"Cassandra might get to model for his new line of perfume," Kerri went on.

"Wow," I said. "That's great, Cassandra."

"It would be a great career move for me right now," said Cassandra, stepping into the red dress. "That's why I have to look just right at this dinner tonight."

"Yeah, I guess what you wear is pretty important," I said. I sighed, thinking of my date with Jordan the next day. "I really need to get some new clothes. None of my stuff is right for New York."

"You're welcome to borrow anything you want," Cassandra said. She rolled up a section of her hair in the curling iron.

"Really?" I said. "Are you sure? Like could I borrow something tomorrow?"

"Of course," she said. "Take whatever you want."

"Where are you going tomorrow?" asked Kerri.

"Well, actually, I kind of have a date," I said. "For lunch."

"Don't tell me!" said Cassandra, turning to face me. "With that guy Jordan?"

"Yeah," I said. Talking about it made me feel fluttery inside again.

"Who's Jordan?" asked Kerri.

"Jordan is this absolutely adorable guy who works at the Cocoa Bean," said Cassandra, as she combed mousse through her hair.

"Oh, you mean that coffee bar you told me about?" asked Kerri.

"That's right," said Cassandra. "Paige, that's great! I knew that guy was nuts about you. How did it happen?"

"Well," I said. "I was walking by there on

my way home from getting my contact lenses..."

"You got them!" said Cassandra. She turned to Kerri. "Pia and I were telling her she really should get contact lenses. She's got such beautiful eyes."

"Definitely," agreed Kerri. "Now you can show them off on your date with Jordan tomorrow. So, tell us more. You were walking by the Cocoa Bean, and what happened?"

"Not much, really," I said. "Jordan saw me, and he came outside, and we started talking. Then he asked me out to lunch tomorrow, and I said yes."

"Not just like that, though," said Cassandra. She opened her eyes wide as she applied mascara. "You told him you had to check your schedule or something first, right?"

"No," I said. "I already *knew* I was free."

Cassandra sighed.

"*You* may have known that, Paige, but you didn't have to let him know it," she said.

"Really," said Kerri. "You should have made him sweat it out a little before you said yes."

"But why?" I asked.

"Why? *Ta brincando?* Are you kidding? Because guys are always more interested when you play hard to get," said Cassandra.

"Always?" I repeated, starting to feel worried.

"Of course," said Kerri. "A guy will always like you more if he thinks you're unavailable. Take me, for instance. There was this guy Kyle at my school in Florida, and I was crazy about him for practically a whole year. I did everything I could think of to make him notice me, but he never really paid any attention. Then, at the end of the year, I started going out with this other guy named Chris, and sure enough, as soon as Kyle realized I was taken, he asked me out."

"Wow," I said.

"That's how guys are," said Cassandra. "The more they think you like them, the less interested they are in you."

"You can't be too nice to them," agreed Kerri. "As soon as you are, it's all over."

"Gosh," I said. "I hope I wasn't too nice to Jordan."

"Don't worry," said Cassandra. "If you

105

were, you can probably still make up for it to-morrow at lunch." She turned to face me. "How do I look?"

"Incredible," I said. It was true. Cassandra's hair and makeup were perfect, and the red dress showed off her figure.

"Okay," she said. "I've got to go. Listen, what time is your date tomorrow, Paige?"

"One o'clock," I answered.

"Great," she said. "That gives us plenty of time in the morning. Let's all meet here at ten-thirty and we can figure out what you're going to wear."

"Ten-thirty!" I said. "But that's two and a half hours! Am I really going to need all that time just to get dressed?"

Cassandra and Kerri looked at each other.

"Believe me," said Cassandra. "Looking good takes time. Besides, something tells me we've got a lot more to work on than just what you're going to wear."

"No kidding," said Kerri. "You've got to learn how you have to act and what to say and stuff."

Suddenly, I felt incredibly relieved. I may have goofed with Jordan today, but Kerri and Cassandra were going to make sure that tomorrow went well.

"Thanks, guys," I said.

That night I lay in bed, tossing and turning, thinking about everything Cassandra and Kerri had said. Was it really true that guys didn't like you if you were nice to them? Had I been too nice to Jordan? Maybe Jordan wasn't like the guys that Cassandra and Kerri knew. But there was no way to be sure.

I kept going over the conversation I'd had with him. I shouldn't have agreed to the date so fast. Now Jordan probably thought I'd been desperate for him to ask me out. Maybe he could even tell that I'd never really been on a date before. I was sure that he'd probably dated lots of really sophisticated New York girls. Girls who didn't have to introduce him to their guardians first. Well, I'd just have to make up for my mistakes tomorrow. I was glad that I had Kerri and Cassandra to help me.

Finally, as the sun was beginning to come up, I drifted off to sleep. But first I promised myself that the next day at lunch Jordan would get to see a new me.

"Oh, forget it," I said. I looked at the mess of clothes strewn about the room. "Maybe I should just wear something of my own."

It was the next day, and I'd been trying on outfits for an hour.

"Come on, Paige," said Cassandra. "You must be more patient. Like I said, looking good takes time. Here, try these." She handed me a pair of black and white striped, cropped leggings.

"I don't know," I said, looking at them doubtfully. "Aren't they a little flashy? I mean, we're just going to lunch."

"Don't forget, you're in New York now," said Kerri. "People dress up more here. Besides, they'll look great on you."

"Here," said Cassandra. She pulled something out of a dresser drawer and tossed it to me. "This is the top that goes with them."

I stepped into the leggings and pulled the matching black and white striped midriff tank top over my head.

"That looks fantastic," said Kerri.

"You look great," agreed Cassandra.

"Are you sure?" I asked, looking down at

the outfit. "I feel like some kind of a zebra in an aerobics class or something."

"Believe me," said Cassandra. "It's very chic." She rummaged through the closet. "Here, try this jacket on."

I took the cropped black linen jacket she handed me and slipped it on over the tank top. I definitely liked the outfit a little more with the jacket on. Still, I couldn't help wishing it were a little longer, so it would cover up some of the pants, too.

"Now," said Cassandra. "What next?" She snapped her fingers. "Shoes!"

"Pia's got the perfect shoes," said Kerri. "She was wearing them yesterday. I'll go and see if we can borrow them."

A minute later, Kerri came back with Pia, who was holding a pair of black platform sandals in her hand.

"*Ma che cosa succede?* What's happening here?" said Pia. "Paige, I hear you have made a date with the handsome coffee boy from the other day!"

I nodded. "We're going out to lunch."

"That is wonderful!" she said. "And you look *fantastica!* But Kerri tells me you need shoes. I will of course be happy to donate

109

mine to this event." She handed me the platform sandals.

"Thanks, Pia," I said, taking them from her.

"Try them on," said Cassandra. "Let's see how they look."

I sat down on the edge of my bed, slipped my feet into the shoes, and stood up. The thick, chunky soles made me feel like I was about a foot taller. I wasn't too sure that I wanted to be a foot taller. I felt too tall to begin with.

"Wow," I said, trying to get my balance. "I don't know if I can walk in these."

"Soon they will feel quite comfortable, you'll see," said Pia.

"Sure," said Kerri. "You just have to practice walking around the apartment in them a little."

"We'd better get started on your hair and makeup," said Cassandra. She looked at her watch. "We only have an hour until he gets here."

"I know," said Pia. "How about a French twist? I wear my hair—I mean, I *used* to wear my hair—that way all the time. It's very elegant." She put her hands up to her ears. "And

110

you can wear these earrings, too. They are perfect with a French twist."

"Great idea," agreed Cassandra. Pia handed me the heavy, dangling silver earrings she had been wearing. "You start on her hair, Pia, and I'll do her makeup."

For the next half an hour I let everyone fuss over me and tell me what to do. My hair was twisted into a pile on top of my head, the earrings were in my ears, and my makeup was finished. I felt as if I were getting ready for another photo shoot. Cassandra had put a lot more makeup on my face than I usually wore, even for special occasions. But I figured she had probably done a good job because everyone insisted that I looked great.

"Now," said Kerri, "time to go over your strategy."

"My strategy?" I repeated.

"Sure," said Kerri. "How you're going to act. What you're going to say. You know, to make sure Jordan stays interested in you."

"Oh, yeah," I said. "Don't be too nice, right?"

"Exactly," said Kerri. "Play it cool. And make sure you drop a few names of other guys you're seeing."

"But I'm not seeing any other guys," I pointed out.

"So?" said Cassandra. "Make some up."

"You have this boy back in Nebraska, no?" asked Pia. "The one you told us about?"

"I suppose," I said. Somehow it seemed wrong to talk about Tommy as if he were a real boyfriend. Especially since I knew that he was taking Kim to the Teen Dance. Still, I guessed I could stretch the truth about Tommy a little if it meant keeping Jordan interested in me.

"Okay," said Cassandra, looking at her watch. "Fifteen minutes to go."

"I guess I'd better practice walking in these shoes," I said. I looked down at the platform sandals. The last thing I wanted to do was to fall on my face in front of Jordan.

I clumped out into the living room with the others behind me. Mrs. Hill was polishing the glass coffee table, and Naira was sitting on the couch, labeling snapshots and gluing them into her New York scrapbook.

"Wow," said Naira, as she looked up. "I hardly recognized you, Paige. You look dressed to kill."

"Yeah, well, I kind of have a date," I told her.

"Must be some date," said Naira. She raised her eyebrows and looked at me expectantly. It made me feel more nervous than I already was.

"This is the boy you told me about, Paige?" asked Mrs. Hill.

"That's right," I said. "He's coming here to pick me up."

"Doesn't she look great?" asked Cassandra. "Those are all my clothes, and Pia's earrings and shoes."

"The shoes look pretty hard to walk in," said Naira. She was still giving me a funny look.

"I know," I said. "I've got to practice before he gets here." I clumped across the floor toward the windows, turned around, and clumped back.

"There," said Pia. "It is getting easier, no?"

I shrugged. The truth was, I felt like I was wearing two big blocks of wood on my feet. And I was starting to realize that the sandals not only were a pain to walk in, but they were also a little tight. I didn't want to say anything and be rude, though. After all, Pia had been nice enough to lend them to me.

"I'm sure I'll be fine," I said. I clumped back and forth across the room a few more times. Everyone watched me, and I felt that it was going as badly as the beginning of the photo shoot.

"Well, I hope you're okay in those shoes, dear," said Mrs. Hill, looking skeptical.

Just then, the doorbell rang, and I froze.

"Oh my gosh, it's him," I said. My heart started to pound.

"Quick, Paige, go!" whispered Kerri, as Mrs. Hill headed toward the door.

"What are you talking about?" I whispered back. "Go where?"

"In the other room!" she hissed.

"Yes, hurry!" said Cassandra. "You have to make him wait a little. You don't want him to think that you've been getting ready for this date all morning, do you?"

Mrs. Hill start to unlock the door and I saw Cassandra's point. As quickly as I could, I turned and ran out of the room, my feet banging loudly across the floor.

CHAPTER 9

Half an hour later, Jordan and I sat across from each other at a small square table with a white lace tablecloth. It was a pretty restaurant, with lots of plants hanging from the ceiling, lace curtains in the windows, and classical music playing in the background.

"So," said Jordan, "you're a model, huh? I guess I should have known, with your pretty face."

I started to smile, but stopped myself. Don't let him know how much that compliment meant to you, I reminded myself. Keep cool.

"Yes," I said with a bored sigh. I shook out the white cloth napkin and put it carefully on my lap. "I'm with Ford Models."

Just a little white lie, I thought. After all, I am *sort of* with Ford.

"And you and your roommates all live in that apartment together, and Mrs. Hill kind of takes care of you, is that it?" he asked.

"That's right," I said, feeling Pia's earrings swing as I nodded. "Ford got the apartment for us."

"That must be kind of fun," said Jordan. "Getting to make friends with people from different countries like that."

"I guess," I said. Then I remembered to try and look like I've known loads of people from all over the world.

"Well, Mrs. Hill seemed really nice," said Jordan.

"She is," I agreed. Then I heard Cassandra's voice in the back of my head. "Actually, it's kind of a pain following all her rules, though," I said. "'Don't do this, don't do that.' At home, my family pretty much let me do whatever I wanted. I really hate having to tell her where I'm going and who I'm with every time I have a date."

"Oh," said Jordan. "Yeah, I guess you must have met a lot of guys since you've been in New York."

He looked kind of disappointed, and for a moment I wished I could just tell him the truth. I don't know any guys in New York, I wanted to say. In fact, I've never even been on a real date before. But I could hear Kerri's and Cassandra's warnings in the back of my head. Don't be too nice—guys always like you more if they think you're not interested.

"Oh, sure," I said, trying to sound casual. "Tons."

"Well," said Jordan quietly, "maybe we should take a look at the menu and decide what we're going to have."

I picked up my menu and opened it. There was a long list of dishes, from hamburgers to much fancier looking stuff. Some of the names of things were in French, and I began to wish I had paid more attention that day we had done the lesson called "At a Restaurant" back in French class at Wheeler High. It would probably make a bigger impression on Jordan if I ordered something in French. Well, at least I knew how to pronounce the names of the French dishes.

I looked down at the little card of daily specials that was attached to the menu.

"Vichyssoise," I read in my best French accent.

"You like that?" asked Jordan.

"Oh, I adore it," I said quickly, wondering what it was. "Really, it's one of my favorites."

"What *is* it?" he asked.

I stared at him.

"Oh, um, what is it?" I stammered. Now I felt really dumb. "Well, it's kind of hard to explain. It's—it's—a French dish, actually."

Jordan shrugged.

"I don't think I'll have it today, though," I mumbled. I looked back down at my menu. All I needed now was to order it and then have it turn out to be something really horrible. As if I hadn't already made enough of a fool of myself.

A moment later, the waiter came to take our order.

"Have you decided, Paige?" asked Jordan.

I scanned the menu, looking for something that was written in English but that would still seem sophisticated.

"Um, I'll have the angel-hair pasta with duck and asparagus in basil cream sauce," I said quickly.

"One angel-hair pasta," said the waiter. "And for the gentleman?"

"I'll take a cheeseburger," said Jordan. "Medium-well, please."

"Certainly," said the waiter. He wrote on his pad and walked away.

"Sorry," said Jordan, smiling at me sheepishly. "I know it probably sounds boring, but I'm not really that into fancy food."

"Are you kidding?" I said. "Cheeseburgers are my favorite."

He looked confused.

"Next to angel-hair pasta," I added quickly.

But when the food got there I began to wish more than ever that I had ordered a cheeseburger, too. My pasta was okay, but the flavors of all the stuff in it were a little weird together, and the cream sauce was incredibly thick and heavy.

"Good?" asked Jordan, biting into his cheeseburger.

"Oh, delicious," I answered. I twirled some more of the sticky pasta on my fork.

"So, Paige, tell me," he said, "where are you from?"

I thought a moment. Wheeler, Nebraska, wasn't exactly a very impressive place to say you were from. But I couldn't exactly lie, either.

"Oh, I'm from the Midwest," I answered, taking another bite of my pasta.

"Really? Where?" asked Jordan.

I swallowed. "Nebraska, actually."

"Nebraska, huh?" said Jordan. "I've never been there. What's it like?"

"Oh, there's really no reason to go there," I answered, shrugging. "It's really boring, you know. Nothing around but miles of cornfields. Of course, I couldn't wait to get out here to New York, where things are really happening."

"I guess," said Jordan. "I grew up not far from here myself, in the suburbs. My dad has an apartment in the city, though. My parents are divorced, and I'm starting college here in the fall, so I'm staying with him."

Suddenly, my mind was filled with questions. What was it like growing up near New York City? How old had he been when his parents got divorced? Was his mother remarried? Did he like living with his father? But I stopped myself. Don't act too interested if you want him to like you, I reminded myself.

"Oh," I said. I tried to regain my bored expression.

"I've been working at the Cocoa Bean this summer to save money for college," Jordan went on. "Last summer I had a job at the beach, as a lifeguard. It was fun, and it was a lot easier sitting in the sun all day than it is waiting tables, but the Cocoa Bean pays better. Besides, being at the beach just made me want to jump in the water. I'm really into swimming; I was on my high-school swim team."

"Oh, really?" I said. I thought about what Kerri had said to me, how I should make sure to mention other guys' names. "This guy I know back in Nebraska, actually, he's, um, one of the guys I go out with there, was the star of our high-school swim team. His name's Tommy—I mean Tom Nelson."

"Oh," said Jordan. He put his napkin on the table. "Listen, maybe we should get the check, and I'll walk you home."

"Okay," I said. I had definitely had enough of my pasta, anyway.

We walked out of the restaurant, with me trying to balance in Pia's clunky shoes. Now I was sure they were at least a size too small, and I could feel blisters starting to form under a couple of the straps. My contact lenses were also beginning to bother me a little. I had begun to notice that if I wore them for too long, my eyes started to feel a little uncomfortable. And all that eye makeup Cassandra had put on me wasn't helping.

Luckily, the restaurant was only a couple of blocks away, so in a few moments, we were standing outside my building.

I looked at Jordan, wondering if he would try to kiss me. My heart pounded at the thought, but I tried to look calm.

"Well," he said. He looked a little uncomfortable. "Thanks a lot, Paige."

"Sure, Jordan," I said, feeling uncomfortable myself. "Thanks for lunch."

"Bye," he said. He looked at me for a moment, his green eyes searching mine. "Take care."

Here it comes, I thought—the kiss. I closed my eyes and waited.

But nothing happened. When I opened my eyes, Jordan was halfway down the block.

That was weird, I thought. I had been so sure he was going to kiss me. Wasn't that what was supposed to happen at the end of a date? I wondered if I had done something wrong. But I had followed Kerri and Cassandra's advice all the way. After all, they were the experts—I was still new at all this stuff. There was probably a logical explanation for Jordan's behavior. I'd just have to ask Kerri and Cassandra about it when I got upstairs.

But when I got up to the apartment, the living room was empty except for Naira, who was on the telephone, her appointment book open in front of her.

"Okay, thanks, Jill," she said, writing in her book. "Two o'clock tomorrow to test. I'll be there."

She hung up the phone.

"Hi, Paige," she said.

"Hi. Where is everyone?" I asked.

"Well, Pia was booked for a shoot all afternoon, and Katerina's been in her room the whole time," she said. "Mrs. Hill went out to do errands, and Kerri and Cassandra went to a shoot too. Then they were planning on going to some spa they found called Jolie."

"A spa?" I said.

"Yeah," said Naira. She didn't sound very impressed. "They're having facials and getting their nails done. I guess they want to look their best for Tuesday."

"What's Tuesday?" I asked.

"All six of us are booked for a photo shoot for *Style* magazine," she said. "It's a winter coat layout for their November issue."

"Wow," I said, "that's great." Not only would I have an opportunity to get more photos for my book, but the photo shoot for *Style* would be my first real booking!

"Yeah," said Naira, "except for the fact that they want us at five o'clock in the morning."

"Five o'clock!" I repeated. "Why so early?"

"It's an outdoor shoot, and the best light for photographs is early morning," Naira explained. "I think they said they're doing the shoot on some rooftop."

"Oh, I get it," I said, nodding.

"So, how was *the* date?" she asked.

I thought about it a moment. I guessed I couldn't exactly say I had had *fun*. I had been far too nervous about remembering to follow Kerri and Cassandra's advice to really enjoy myself. But I *had* managed to keep cool, and hopefully it kept Jordan interested. Something about the way the date had ended still nagged at me, though.

"Naira," I said, "can I ask you something?"

"Shoot."

"What would you think if a guy seemed like he really liked you when you first met, but then at the end of the first date he didn't try to kiss you or ask you out again or any-thing?"

"Well," she said. She paused for a second and looked thoughtful. "I'm not sure. I guess it would depend on the guy. Maybe he didn't think we got along. If it really seemed like he liked me, though, I'd probably just think he was kind of shy. He might even need a little push in the right direction, you know what I mean, a little...encouragement."

I sighed. *Encouragement!* How was I sup-posed to encourage Jordan *and* play it cool at the same time? I shook my head. This guy stuff was starting to seem way too compli-cated.

CHAPTER 10

"Okay, girls!" Simone Grey called from behind her camera. "Let's try that again."

The six of us turned and walked away from the camera, back toward the low, brick wall that ran around the edge of the roof.

"Phew!" said Naira under her breath. "I'm boiling."

I knew what she meant. It was Tuesday, and we had been up on the roof of an apartment building for about an hour in the sun, dressed in winter parkas, hats, scarves, and gloves. At least it was early, so it was a little cooler, but still I was starting to sweat under the puffy cream-colored parka and long, striped stocking cap that Linda, the stylist, had dressed me in.

On top of wearing clothes meant for Alaska, Simone, the photographer, wanted a shot of us all running together in a line, arm in arm. I felt like we had jogged by the camera about a million times already. It was getting harder and harder to look as bouncy and happy as Simone wanted us to be. Of course, she was dressed in cut-off shorts and a tank top with her shoulder-length hair tucked up into a baseball cap.

I took my place between Naira, in her red parka and white earmuffs, and Katerina, who was dressed in a green parka trimmed with black fake fur, and we linked arms. Naira linked arms with Kerri, who linked arms with Cassandra, who linked arms with Pia.

"Ready?" called Simone. "Okay, go!"

We took off, trotting across the roof toward the camera.

"All right, girls, that wasn't bad, but I'd like to try it again. You all need to look like you're jogging to keep warm, so try and look a little cold, but not *too* cold," said Simone. "And you on the end—what's your name, in the green?"

"Katerina," Katerina answered quietly.

"Yes, Katerina," Simone said. "This time, I'd like you to try to loosen up a little. Smile, look like you're having fun."

Boy, does *that* sound familiar, I thought, walking back to the edge of the roof with the others.

"Okay, let's go!" Simone called.

We linked arms again and began jogging.

"Hold on, hold on!" shouted Simone. "I don't think we had the light on that one." She turned to her assistant, who was standing a few feet away. He was holding a big piece of metallic silver board. "Mark, keep that reflector moving as the models move," she said. "Make sure you keep the light on them all the time."

"Okay," said Mark, nodding and adjusting the silver piece so that it reflected the sun directly into my face. "Sorry."

"All right, let's try it again," said Simone. "Makeup, I think the girl in the white needs some powder. She's shining a little."

Who wouldn't be, I thought, as the makeup woman walked up to me and brushed some powder onto my nose and cheeks. In this heat, I was surprised my whole face wasn't melting. It was amazing how much harder modeling was turning out to be than I had ever expected. I had thought all models had to do was look good and smile. This was worse than the acting class I'd taken my fresh-man year at Wheeler High.

"Okay, good," said Simone.

We all turned and walked back to the edge of the roof.

"I feel like I'm playing Red Light, Green Light," joked Kerri. She unzipped her powder blue parka a little and loosened her white knit scarf.

I laughed.

"What is this 'Red-Green Light?'" asked Pia, tossing the end of her multicolored scarf over her yellow parka.

"Red Light, Green Light. It's a running game that kids play," explained Naira. "If you're caught moving, you have to go back to the starting line."

"Ah, *si*, I think I understand," said Pia. "We play a similar game in Italy."

That's pretty interesting, I thought. I guess kids like to do the same kinds of things all over.

"Hold on a sec!" called Linda, the stylist. She hurried over to Kerri and rezipped her jacket, tightening her scarf.

Kerri sighed and shrugged. "It was worth a try," she said, winking at us.

"Ready?" Simone called. "Okay, let's go! Smile, Katerina. Remember, you're having fun!"

Katerina stiffened a little on my right. As we jogged, I could tell that she wasn't in step with the rest of us. It seemed strange, especially since she usually moved so gracefully. I wondered what was going on.

"Okay, wait!" called Simone. "Hold on! Katerina, your face was a little better on that one, but you need to relax your body more, okay?"

Katerina didn't say anything, just turned and walked back to the edge of the roof with the rest of us, her chin in the air. But as we took our places again and I linked my arm through hers, I noticed something peculiar. She was shivering, almost as if she were cold! First I thought that she was doing it to make Simone happy. Then I thought, no way, she's really shaking. But how could anyone be shivering dressed like that in the hot sun? Maybe she wasn't feeling well. I looked at her trying to figure out what was going on. She avoided my eye by staring intently at the horizon, her lips pressed together.

Simone tried the shot a few more times and then told us to stop for a moment.

"I'd like to make a couple of changes," she said, putting her camera down. "First, Katerina, we're going to give you a little break for a couple of minutes."

"Oh, but Simone," said Linda, "I really think we need her green jacket in this shot."

"Well, then, put it on someone else," said Simone. She looked at us. "Try it on the redhead—it'll look great with her hair."

"Good idea," said Linda. "Katerina, give your jacket to the girl next to you, would you?"

I looked at Katerina and saw that her face was bright red. In one quick movement, she unzipped her green jacket, yanked it off, and pushed it into my arms. Then, without saying a word, she raised her chin and turned around. We all watched in shocked silence as she stalked across the roof toward the door that led downstairs. Then she pulled open the door and marched through it, letting it slam behind her.

We all looked at each other in amazement. Even Simone and Linda looked surprised.

"*Eh! Caspita!*" exclaimed Pia.

"Can you believe that?" Cassandra shook her head.

"That girl has a real attitude problem," commented Kerri.

"All right, all right, that's enough," said Simone. "Linda, let's finish setting this next shot. I want the redhead and the two girls next to her for this one. Mark, why don't you go downstairs and see if you can find Katerina."

"Sure," said Mark. He put down the reflector and headed through the door.

"Okay," said Simone. "Let's keep working. You two," she pointed at Pia and Cassandra, "you can take your jackets off and relax for a couple of minutes. I've got a shot in mind for you with Katerina when she gets back. Linda, see what you want to do with the other three."

Five minutes later, Linda had switched around all of our outfits. Now I was in the green jacket that Katerina had been wearing, along with Naira's white earmuffs. Naira was wearing Pia's yellow parka with my stocking cap, and Kerri had kept her powder blue parka but Linda had added a pink knit headband.

"Okay," said Linda. "They're ready."

Just then, Mark came back up to the roof.

"Sorry, Simone, I can't find her," he said. "I think she might have left."

"*Left?*" said Simone. "She can't do that. I wasn't finished working with her." She shook her head. "I had a shot in mind for her with those other two."

Kerri shot Cassandra a look. "Can you believe she did that?" she whispered.

Cassandra rolled her eyes. "How unprofessional."

"Okay, let's not let this slow us down," said Simone. "Back to work."

For the next hour or so, Simone called out directions to Kerri, Naira, and me. She took pictures of us standing and talking together, pictures of us holding hands and jumping up in the air, pictures of us sitting on the wall at the edge of the roof, and pictures of us huddled together as if we were cold. I didn't know which was harder, sitting near the edge of the roof like that without feeling dizzy, or trying to pretend I was freezing when it was at least 80 degrees out.

At least I could tell that I was doing a better job this time than I had with Will Nichols.

133

I was much more relaxed, and a couple of times I actually even started to have fun, instead of just trying to look that way. Naira and Kerri helped me feel more comfortable by cracking jokes and goofing around. And whenever I started to feel self-conscious, I tried to think of the pond, the way Will Nichols had taught me.

The contact lenses made it easier, too, because now I could see what was going on around me. I still wasn't quite used to them but I hadn't really realized how unsure of myself it had made me feel at the first shoot to have everything around me looking blurry.

After Simone Grey was finished with us, she took some shots of Cassandra and Pia, and then a few of the five of us together. But all through the rest of the shoot I was thinking of Katerina and the way she had stormed off like that. It sure was a strange thing to do. I mean, there were times at the test with Will Nichols when I had just felt like giving up, but I never would have had the guts to make a big scene like that.

Finally, it was almost ten o'clock, and Simone said she was finished with us. I couldn't believe it. Only ten o'clock in the morning, and I had already worked a five-hour day! But in its own way, it was like being back at the farm. My family always got up early to do the chores, and then we'd all meet back at the house for one of my mother's big breakfasts.

"*Allora,* well, who is ready for a coffee at the Cocoa Bean?" asked Pia, when the five of us got outside on the sidewalk.

"Me," sighed Cassandra. "I need a large *cafezinho.*"

"Sounds good to me, too," agreed Naira.

"And I want to check out this Cocoa Bean place," said Kerri. She grinned. "Not to mention Paige's new boyfriend."

"He's not really my boyfriend," I said. "I mean, we've only had one date."

"So far," pointed out Cassandra.

"Yeah," I sighed. "And I'm beginning to wonder if there's ever going to be another."

"Why?" asked Kerri. "Didn't things work out?" She looked at me. "Paige, you followed our advice, didn't you?"

"What advice?" asked Naira.

"I did!" I answered. "I did everything you guys told me to, I promise."

"Then you have nothing to worry about," said Cassandra. She turned to Naira. "Kerri and I told Paige that she shouldn't act too crazy about this guy Jordan if she wanted to keep him interested in her."

"Ah, *si*, this is true," agreed Pia. "Many boys are like this. Sometimes they like you to play—how you say—hard to gain."

"Hard to get," Naira corrected. "But it totally depends on the guy. I mean, sure, *some* boys are like that…"

"Believe me," Kerri interrupted, rolling her eyes, "they're all the same. So, where's this Cocoa Bean place, anyway?"

Ten minutes later the Cocoa Bean came into view. The closer we got, the more nervous I felt. Maybe this wasn't a good idea. Maybe I should just wait for Jordan to call me or something.

"You guys," I said, stopping. "Hold on. I don't know if I want to go."

"What?" said Pia. "Why not, Paige? Don't you want to see Jordan again?"

"Well, sure," I answered. "But what if *he* doesn't want to see *me* again?"

"Don't be silly, Paige," said Kerri. "He's probably dying for you to come in."

"But if he likes me so much, why didn't he ask me out on another date?" I asked.

"Don't worry about it," said Cassandra. "He's probably just trying to play it cool, too. Don't you see? It's like a game."

"A game?" I repeated.

"Sure," said Kerri. "It's all strategy. First he makes his move, then you make yours, and so on. Neither of you give away your final game plan."

I looked at Naira. She'd hardly said a word throughout the whole conversation. I couldn't help wondering if she agreed with the others. She seemed so sensible.

"What do you think?" I asked her.

"I don't know," she said. "I've never even met this guy. But you should never feel intimidated about going somewhere just because you think someone else might be there. Why should this guy ruin your morning, whoever he is? If you feel like going to the Cocoa Bean, go to the Cocoa Bean."

I nodded. That made sense.

Until I walked into the Cocoa Bean, that is. The moment I saw Jordan, all my old nervousness came back. The place was pretty crowded, and he was up at the counter with his back to us, so he hadn't seen me yet. It was all I could do to keep from running out of there before he turned around.

"That is him, over there," Pia whispered loudly.

"Oooh, he looks cute," said Kerri. "Now, remember, Paige, play it cool. Act like you don't notice him at first."

As we sat down at one of the round tables, I could feel my heart pounding. Afraid to look up, I kept my eyes fixed on the green marble surface of the table. I wondered if he had seen me yet, and what I should do.

Suddenly, I heard his voice.

"May I take your order?"

I looked up and our eyes met for a moment.

"Hi, Paige," he said. "How are you?"

"Fine, thanks," I answered, my throat tight.

"What can I get you?" he asked, looking back down at his order pad.

"I think I'd like to have the iced choco-cappuccino," I said. I tried to smile.

But Jordan just scribbled my order on his pad.

"Okay," he said, turning to Naira. "And for you?"

"A cup of regular," said Naira.

I watched as he took everyone's order, the

expression on his face unchanged. I was beginning to wish I had left when I had the chance. It was pretty clear that Jordan didn't care about seeing me again. I watched, dejected, as he walked away to get our drinks.

"You see, you guys?" I said. "This was definitely a mistake. He hates me."

"You don't know that for sure," said Pia. "Perhaps it is just as Cassandra said, that he is simply playing the game with you."

"She's right," said Kerri. "He's probably just trying to show you he can be cool, too."

"I guess," I said. But suddenly I felt pretty fed up with games and playing it cool. Maybe this was how they did things in New York, but if so, I'd take Wheeler any day.

I sighed.

"Don't look so glum," said Cassandra. "There are plenty of other guys out there."

"Really, Paige," said Pia. "Right now you have an expression on your face like that of Katerina."

Kerri shook her head. "Boy, what was *her* problem today?"

"I think she was upset about something," said Naira.

"That is for sure," said Pia.

"I bet she got angry just because she couldn't be in every shot," said Cassandra.

"Yes," said Pia. "I am beginning to think she is—how you say—a bit of a snob, no?"

"I don't know, guys," I said. "There may be more to it than that. I noticed that even before she left, when we were linking arms, she was kind of shaking."

"Shaking?" asked Naira. "What do you mean?"

"I don't know," I said. "It was almost like she was shivering or something."

"Shivering?" repeated Kerri. "In that heat?"

"What's *that* supposed to mean?" asked Cassandra.

"I'll tell you what it means," said Kerri, shaking her head. "It means not only is she a snob, but she's totally strange, too."

Cassandra laughed. "I guess you're right, Kerri."

But I was starting to wonder if Kerri and Cassandra *were* right about Katerina. In fact, I was starting to wonder how right they were about a lot of things.

CHAPTER 11

I wish that I hadn't stopped in at the Cocoa Bean yesterday. It was obvious that Jordan wasn't too pleased to see me. He treated me like just another customer. Besides, it's been four days since our date. He would have asked me out again by now if he were still interested, so I guess he's not.

I just can't figure out what went wrong. I really felt like there was something special between us when we first met. But I guess I had the wrong idea.

I really miss home. I can't believe I've only been away for a little over a week—it feels like way longer. I want to just curl up with Scooter on my own bed in my own room back in Wheeler.

Who knows, I could even be back in Wheeler in three days. I've got plane reservations for

Saturday, and if the Fords haven't offered to take me on by then, I guess I'll head home. I'll get there just in time for school to start on Monday. I still can't help hoping I get to stay, though. Despite the fact that things didn't work out with Jordan, there is something about New York that I really like. And I feel like I'm really starting to get the hang of this modeling stuff.

Just then, there was a knock on the door.

"Come in!" I called. I quickly closed my diary and slipped it under my pillow.

"Hi," said Kerri, poking her head in. "Where's Cassandra?"

"She had a booking," I said.

"Oh, well, I just stopped by to see if you guys wanted to go out for coffee," said Kerri.

"At the Cocoa Bean?" I said. "Thanks, but no thanks."

"Come on, Paige," said Kerri. "You're not still upset about that Jordan guy, are you?"

"Kerri," I said, looking at her. "Don't you dare try to tell me he's playing hard to get. He's just not interested, and that's that."

"Oh, well," said Kerri with a shrug. "Even if that's true, you shouldn't let it get you down so much. After all, New York's a big city. Believe me, there are *plenty* of cute guys out there."

"I suppose," I said. But I tried to ignore the sharp feeling that suddenly appeared in my chest. I wasn't interested in other guys—I liked Jordan.

"Hey, maybe we'll even meet some guys at the Cocoa Bean," said Kerri. "Now, that would show Jordan a thing or two, wouldn't it?"

I sighed. I was tired of trying to show Jordan anything, tired of thinking about acting and looking the right way to keep him interested.

"Kerri, why don't you just go without me," I said.

Kerri looked serious.

"I can't," she said in a low voice.

"What do you mean?" I asked. "Just go alone. Like you said, maybe you'll meet someone when you get there."

"No, you don't understand," she said, almost pleading now. "I *can't.*"

"Why not?" I asked.

Kerri stepped into the room and closed the door behind her.

"Because I don't know how to get there," she said quietly.

"But it's only a few blocks away," I told her.

"I know," she said. "But I also know I'll never find it on my own. The truth is, I can't find my way anywhere in this city by myself. It's so confusing—all the streets look alike to me. I'm too embarrassed to stop anyone and ask for directions, and the more Carla explains things to us, the more confused I get."

"Gosh," I said, looking at her in surprise. "I had no idea." Kerri had always seemed so sure of herself. But come to think of it, I had never seen her go off anywhere alone.

"I have this terrible fear I'm going to get totally lost," she said. "Sometimes I even have nightmares about it. I know I have to get over it if I want to live here, but I don't know what to do."

"Well, you should probably start with something small and simple," I said. "To prove to yourself that you can do it. I'll tell you what—why don't I draw you a really good map showing exactly how to get to the Cocoa Bean? It's really only a few blocks away."

"I don't know..." she began.

"Look, Kerri, take some change with you and you can call me if you get lost," I said.

"Well," she said. "I guess I could try."

I pulled my diary out from under my pillow and ripped out a blank page near the end. I drew a detailed map of how to get from the apartment to the Cocoa Bean, then handed it to Kerri.

"There you go," I said. "Don't forget to take a quarter."

"Thanks, Paige," said Kerri. She paused at the door. "Oh, and Paige?"

"Yes?"

"You won't tell anyone else about this, will you?" she asked. "I mean, it's kind of embarrassing."

"Don't worry," I said. "Your secret is safe with me, Kerri."

Boy, I thought to myself, that was a surprise. Who would have guessed that confident, outgoing Kerri was secretly terrified of getting around New York?

I reached under my bed to put my diary back in my suitcase. As I did, my hand brushed something small and heavy—one of Pia's shoes. I had forgotten to return them the other day after my date with Jordan, and they must have gotten kicked under the bed. And I still had her earrings on my night table, too.

I scooped up the shoes and the earrings

and walked down the hall to Pia and Katerina's room. I knocked lightly on the door, but there was no answer. I'll just leave these things in her room for her, I decided.

I turned the knob and pushed open the door, only to find Katerina standing by one of the dressers with her back to me. She hadn't been around for dinner the night before. Mrs. Hill told us that Katerina had gone to her aunt's house in Brooklyn. Actually I hadn't seen her at all since she'd walked out of yesterday's shoot.

Now she was dressed in a black leotard and tights, with a pair of headphones on her ears. A cassette deck lay on the dresser near her, and she was holding onto the dresser with one hand, kicking the opposite leg out to the side.

I still couldn't get over how gracefully she moved. Her long leg lifted smoothly off the ground, toe pointed, and almost reached her ear before returning silently to the floor. Her back was straight and her neck looked long and elegant.

Suddenly, she caught my eye in the mirror above the dresser. An angry look crossed her face and she tore the headphones off her ears.

"*Ach! Shto-to-yest?* What are you doing here?" she demanded.

"Gee, sorry, Katerina," I said. "I didn't mean to startle you. I'm just returning some things of Pia's."

"Well, then, why did you not knock?" she asked, still scowling.

"I did knock, but there was no answer," I said. "You must not have heard me with your headphones on."

"Oh," she said. She lowered her voice and looked down. "But you did not have to stand there and spy on me, did you?"

"I said I was sorry. I really didn't mean to intrude," I said. "It's just that you looked so— I don't know, *elegant*."

"*Elegant?*" she repeated, her blue eyes flashing. "Ha! That is a good joke."

"What are you talking about?" I asked. "You're very graceful. And you're the most limber person I've ever seen."

"Oh," she said. "You mean the dancing. Sure, I can dance, but that's all."

"What do you mean?" I asked.

She looked at me, and her face darkened. "Why do you not ask Simone Grey? She did not think I could do anything right at all.

147

That is why she decided to leave me out of all the photographs yesterday."

"She wasn't going to leave you out of all of them," I said. "She just didn't need you for a little while. Believe me, she was going to use you later."

Katerina looked at me, her chin jutted out. I couldn't believe it, but she almost looked like she was going to cry.

"How can I believe that, after all those terrible things she said?" she asked, her voice trembling.

It seemed strange that she was so upset about what had happened with Simone. After all, I thought she'd been on hundreds of other shoots.

"What terrible things?" I said. "All right, so she gave you some suggestions and criticisms. Look, you can't take that kind of stuff personally."

"*Prazda!* Sure, that is easy for you to say," she said. "Your modeling career is already started." She looked down. "I have not even been taken on by Ford yet."

"Katerina," I said, almost laughing now, "neither have I!"

She looked at me in surprise. "You haven't?

But I thought—but you seemed to know what to do at the shoot yesterday."

"Yesterday was only my fourth time in front of a camera," I told her. "And you should have seen my first time. I was a mess."

"Yes?" she asked.

"Definitely yes!" I answered. "That photographer was constantly correcting me. 'Paige, relax! Paige, try to look like you're enjoying yourself!' Believe me, I thought I was a total failure as a model."

"That is how I feel," she said. "Ford sent me to test with another photographer a few days ago, and none of the pictures were good because I was too nervous. Jill said we cannot even put them in my book. So yesterday I was terrified that if I did not do well, Ford would refuse to take me on, and I would have to go back to Russia."

"So that's why you were shaking so much," I said. "And that's why you left."

"Yes," she said. "I knew I was ruining everything. I didn't want anyone to see how upset I was." She sighed. "I feel like things are bad enough here for me as it is."

"What do you mean?" I asked.

"Oh, you know. The other girls," she said.

"None of them like me. I can tell."

She blinked back tears. Suddenly, I felt really sorry for her.

"I think they just don't understand you, Katerina," I said. "You see, when you keep quiet and don't show or tell people what you're feeling, then they don't know what you're really like inside. And if they don't know who you are at all, then it's easy for them to get the wrong idea."

"I guess perhaps you are right, Paige," she said. "But now what am I to do about Ford? I am certain that Jill is angry with me for walking out of the shoot. She called here twice yesterday while I was out visiting my aunt, but I have been too frightened to call her back."

"You'll just have to try to explain it to her," I said. "Tell her how sorry you are, and promise never to let it happen again. Perhaps she'll be willing to give you a second chance."

"All right, Paige," said Katerina. "I will try."

"Good." I looked down at the shoes and the earrings in my hands. "Now, where should I leave these things for Pia?"

"I think she keeps her jewelry in that case over there," said Katerina. She pointed to a purple satin box on the opposite dresser. "And the shoes you can put in her side of the closet, on the right."

I walked over to the dresser and opened the purple box. To my surprise, lying among the earrings, bracelets, and necklaces inside was a long lock of thick brown hair, tied at either end with two red ribbons.

"Wow," I said, under my breath. This had to be Pia's hair. She must have taken it from the floor of Will Nichols's studio that day after her haircut. It was funny, though. She hadn't said anything to me or Cassandra about it.

I thought about the strange look Pia had had on her face while her hair was being cut. Then I remembered that day on the Circle Line, when she had explained to Naira and me about her secret olive oil method. Her long hair must have really meant a lot to her, I realized. And even though she had acted like it wasn't a really big deal to get it cut, it must have been hard. She just hadn't let on how she really felt.

"Paige," said Katerina, interrupting my thoughts. "I want to ask you something."

"Sure," I said. I laid the earrings near the

151

lock of hair and carefully closed the purple box. "What is it?"

"It's about the other girls," she said. "What you said—that maybe they misunderstand me. That maybe it's not really that they just don't like me." She took a deep breath. "I wonder, what do you think I should do?"

"That's easy, Katerina," I said, looking at her. "Just be yourself."

Suddenly, everything that had happened with Jordan started to click into place and make sense to me.

The really sad thing was, it was too late.

CHAPTER 12

I was making my way down the hall from Katerina's room as the phone started ringing.

"Paige!" Mrs. Hill called out from the kitchen. "Paige, it's Kerri on the phone for you!"

Uh-oh, I thought as I walked into the living room—I guess maybe she got lost after all.

"I've got it!" I called, picking up the receiver. "Kerri? It's me. Is everything okay?"

"Just great," said Kerri cheerfully. "Guess where I am?"

"The Cocoa Bean?"

"That's right," she said. "I made it. Your map was great, Paige."

"That's wonderful, Kerri," I said. "I knew you could do it on your own."

"Yeah," said Kerri. "Thanks. The funny thing is, you could have come after all. It

153

turns out that guy Jordan isn't even working today."

"Oh," I said. "I guess so." But I had a funny feeling I wouldn't be going to the Cocoa Bean at all anymore. Even if Jordan weren't there, it would only remind me of him and of how stupid I'd been.

"Okay," said Kerri, "I guess I'm going to go have something to celebrate finding my way. Hey, what was that drink you had here yesterday? It looked really good."

"Iced choco-cappuccino," I said, feeling a lump form in my throat.

"Great," she answered. "I think I'll try it."

"Yeah," I said quietly. "Be sure to ask for some whipped cream and cinnamon."

"Okay," said Kerri. "See you later, Paige."

"Bye."

As I hung up the phone, I suddenly wanted to get out of the apartment and go somewhere. But where? I was starting to feel like the only places in New York were coffee bars, trendy cafes, and restaurants with menus written in French. What I really wanted was to go somewhere where I could just feel like me—the *old* me.

Then I got an idea. I hurried back to my

room and put on my faded jeans and an old gray T-shirt. Popping out my contact lenses, I dug into my night-table drawer for my glasses and slipped them on. Finally, I pulled my hair back into a ponytail and slipped my feet into my sneakers. I knew just where I wanted to go—it was a place I had always gone to in Wheeler when I was feeling down and wanted to clear my mind. And now it would be a place where I could forget about New York and modeling and everything else for a while.

"Mrs. Hill?" I called. "Can you tell me where the library is?"

A little while later, I headed up the stone steps of the closest city library and pulled open the door. That familiar library smell hit my nose, and I started to feel better right away. At home the library had always been one of my favorite places. Something about the cool, quiet tables and the shelves of books always seemed to soothe me.

I walked inside and looked around at the long tables filled with people reading and the endless shelves of books. I thought of how impressed Mrs. Johnson back at the Wheeler Library would be by the size of this place.

I made my way through the room, wandering through the stacks of books. I have a funny method in libraries. I like to just walk around first, taking down any books that catch my eye, anything that looks interesting. When I have a bunch of them, I bring them all to one of the tables and sort through them, picking out the ones I think I might want to read.

The selection at this library was bigger than at the one in Wheeler. This time I mostly chose things that had characters who lived in some other time and place. When I'm feeling down I like to lose myself in books about stuff totally unlike my own life. Before I knew it I had a huge stack of books in my arms. It was time to go sit down.

I staggered toward the nearest table, balancing my tower of books. Just as I got there, my sneaker caught on something, and I tripped and fell to my knees, sending all of the books flying.

Unfortunately my glasses stayed on, so that when I looked up, face burning, I could see everyone within earshot staring at me. Great, I thought, so much for making myself feel better by coming to the library.

But suddenly, I recognized one of the people looking at me. I couldn't believe it.

"Jordan?" I said.

"Paige?" he said, looking amazed.

Jordan was sitting in front of a big pile of books, with one of them open on the desk in front of him.

"Here, let me help you," he said. He hurried over to where I was half-sprawled on the ground. "Gosh, I hardly recognized you."

I looked down at my jeans and T-shirt, thought of my glasses and ponytail, and shrugged. "It's me."

"Are all these books yours?" he asked, helping me gather them into a pile and put them on the table.

"Yes," I answered. "I was about to go through them and pick which ones I want to read."

"Wow," he said, as we stood up together. "I have to say, I'm kind of surprised to see you here."

"Ssshhhh!" whispered an old man at the table.

"You are?" I whispered. I added some books to the pile on the table.

"Yeah. You didn't really seem like the library type to me," said Jordan. "You seemed more like the type who spends her time going out. You know, dating and stuff."

I looked at him. Here was my chance to clear things up, to be honest with him. If Jordan didn't like the real me, that was just too bad.

I took a deep breath.

"Jordan," I said. "I have to tell you something."

"Sure, Paige," he said. "What is it?"

"None of that stuff I told you about dating other guys was true," I said. "I made it up because I was trying to impress you."

"*Impress* me?" Jordan repeated.

"Sssssshhhhhh!" The old man was getting angry now.

Jordan lowered his voice.

"Impress me?" he said again. "Don't tell me you actually thought I would *like* the idea that you had tons of other dates?"

I shrugged. "I know, it sounds pretty silly, but I was afraid if you knew the truth, you might not like me."

"The truth?"

I looked at him. "Yes," I said. "The truth. And the truth is that having lunch with you was the first real date I ever went on in my entire life."

Jordan raised his eyebrows. "Then what was all that stuff about that guy back in Nebraska, Mr. Swim Team?"

"Oh, he's a friend, a *good* friend, but still just a friend," I answered. "His family lives on the farm next to mine. We grew up together. I was making a lot more out of it than there ever was."

"Sssssshhhhhh!" said the old man again, wagging a finger at us. "If you two kids want to talk you should go outside. Don't you know this is a library?"

Jordan and I looked at each other and tried not to laugh.

"Good idea," said Jordan. "Hey, listen, how'd you like to go out on the second date of your entire life?"

"I'd love to," I answered.

"So, where to?" asked Jordan, when we got outside the library. "Do you want another iced choco-cappuccino? Or should we go have the real thing?"

"The real thing?" I repeated.

"Yeah," said Jordan, grinning. "A *real*

chocolate soda—with none of that coffee stuff in it."

"Sounds great," I said.

"Okay," he said. "I know a diner near here with a real old-fashioned soda fountain."

"Perfect," I said. "Do they have cheeseburgers, too?"

"The best," said Jordan. "But are you sure you wouldn't rather go somewhere where you can get some cold potato soup?"

"Ick!" I said. "Why would I want that?"

He looked at me and raised an eyebrow. "Vichyssoise," he said. "That French dish you said you loved. I was curious, so I looked it up, and that's what it is—cold potato soup."

"Forget it," I said. "I'll take a chocolate soda and a cheeseburger any day." I thought a moment and smiled. "And I know the perfect place for us to go afterward, too."

"Come on," Jordan said later, taking my hand as we climbed aboard. "Let's get a seat up front, where we can really see the view."

"I don't know," I said. I suddenly felt a little nervous. "I'm not sure I *want* to see."

"Hey, come on, it's no fun unless you look

down," said Jordan. "Besides, this is *your* idea."

"Okay, okay," I said, as he pulled me to the front of the tram.

"Roosevelt Island!" called the conductor. Then he pulled shut the sliding doors to the little red car.

Jordan leaned over to me.

"Here goes," he whispered into my ear.

The tram started with a lurch and then began to glide smoothly out of the station. As it climbed, I could see the cars and taxis and people growing smaller on the street below us. The bridge was to our right, and I knew that Ford was somewhere below.

As the tram climbed higher into the sky, I got a funny feeling in my stomach. But it was impossible to tell whether it was from being so high up or from sitting next to Jordan.

Soon, we were gliding out over the river. The water sparkled below us, and I could see a Circle Line boat sailing along.

"How do you like it?" asked Jordan as he leaned toward me.

"It's great," I answered.

"It sure is," he said. I turned to look at him

and our eyes met. "Hey!" he said, suddenly. "*That's* it! That's what was missing that day I asked you out to lunch."

"What?" I asked.

"Your glasses."

"Oh, yeah," I said. "I was wearing my contacts. I had just gotten them."

"But you had your glasses on the day I met you," he said. "I remember I noticed them right away because they were all taped up on one side."

"I know," I said, laughing. "I guess I must have looked pretty silly."

"I thought you looked great," he said. "The tape on your glasses was kind of cute. In fact, it was one of the first things I noticed about you."

"Really?" I said.

"Sure," he said. "It kind of set you apart, made you seem different from everyone else in there."

"So you *liked* my broken glasses?" I repeated. *This* I couldn't believe.

"Paige," he said, leaning closer to kiss me, "I liked *you*."

CHAPTER 13

Well, now its Saturday, the night of the Teen Dance in Wheeler, and I'm still in New York. It's funny the way things work out. Three days ago, when I was feeling so down, I never would have guessed that it would end up being one of the best days of my life. First, that I'd end up running into Jordan in the library, and then that there'd be a message waiting for me from Eileen Ford when I got back to the apartment.

It really made me feel great when Eileen said that they'd decided to make me a full-fledged Ford model. We sat in her office and looked at my book together, and she told me to think it over carefully and served me some chamomile tea ("Good for helping you make decisions," she said). I didn't have to think about it too much, though. I knew I wanted to stay in New York and model.

I know I'll miss my family a lot, but I'm also incredibly excited about starting my new life here in New York. Having a friend like Jordan is going to help, too. I'm so glad things got straightened out between us.

When I talked to my mom the other night, she said she was packing up more of my clothes and stuff to send me. She also said she was sending me a surprise by special air cargo delivery right away. The package arrived today, and guess what was inside? Scooter!

It's so great to have him here. Everyone seems to like him, and Mrs. Hill said it was fine to keep him as long as I take care of him. I thought it might be a big adjustment for him in New York, but so far he seems to like it just fine. In fact, he spends most of his time looking out the window at the river, watching the boats go by.

After Scooter arrived, there was only one thing I still had to do to make this place feel like home, and that was unpack Mr. Wigglesworth and put him on my bed. What amazed me was the way Cassandra reacted when she saw him. I was totally shocked when she ran over to him and picked him up. It turns out she had a stuffed bunny when she was just a kid, and that one of her family's maids accidentally threw it out. As she told me the story she practically got tears in her eyes!

Then we got to talking, and she told me that she didn't get the Milo Manning perfume job after all. I could tell she was pretty disappointed, but she's one of those people who always bounces right back. Rather than quitting, I think it makes her more determined.

It's funny how often people seem to keep their feelings hidden inside. First there was Kerri and her fear of getting lost, and then Katerina and her worries about modeling (luckily, she convinced the Fords to give her another chance). And then there was Pia and her hair, and now Cassandra. Maybe everyone has something they feel a little insecure about deep down.

I guess sometimes you just can't tell what people are like on the inside by the way they seem on the outside. One thing I know now for sure—from this day on, I'm just going to be me, Paige Sanders.

WORDS EVERY MODEL SHOULD KNOW

book (or **portfolio**): a collection of a model's current photos and tear sheets. Clients look at these books to choose the models they want to hire. A model's book can make or break her career.

booker (or **agent**): the person responsible for a model's day-to-day schedule. Bookers may speak to their models as often as ten times a day!

booking: a scheduled modeling job.

client: a company, magazine, or photographer who hires a model.

editorial shoot: a modeling job for a fashion magazine.

location: where a shoot takes place.

option: an unconfirmed booking.

shoot: a photo session.

stylist: a person who chooses the clothes and accessories for a shoot.

tear sheets: pages with photos from a model's editorial shoots, these are torn from magazines and put in a model's book. The more well-known the magazines and photographers, the more impressive the tear sheets.

test shoot: a shoot at which a starting model has photos taken for her book. A model isn't paid for a test shoot because the modeling agency hires the photographers and stylists.

Don't miss SUPERMODELS OF THE WORLD™ 2: PARTY GIRL
Available now from Red Fox, priced £1.99

Cassandra's having the time of her life in New York, but will she jet-set her way out of her modelling contract?

"First, I'd like to welcome each and every one of you to the Supermodel of the World Contest," said Eileen Ford.

I sat up straighter and shook my hair into place. I knew this was an important moment in my career, a chance to get Eileen and Jerry Ford, the heads of New York City's prestigious Ford Models, to notice me in the crowd. But it wasn't going to be easy—I was surrounded by some of the most beautiful girls in the world.

It was the first day of the week-long Supermodel of the World Contest. All the contestants were sitting in the garden of the Ocean Plaza Hotel on the tropical island of Luzia, where the contest was going to take place. The Fords stood in front of us, Jerry in a dark suit and Eileen in a beige skirt and sweater, her glasses pushed up into her short light hair.

I'd met the Fords once before, when I won the local modeling contest in my country, Brazil. This was different. This was the international contest. Now I was competing with models from all over the world. Winning the contest was a long shot, but I was <u>determined</u> to make an impression on the Fords. It was my big chance, the first step toward becoming a Ford model in New York City.

"During the week," said Jerry, "you'll all have an opportunity to work with top photographers and fashion designers..."

I shivered. I knew this was the break I needed. I'd already modeled back in Rio de Janeiro, the city where I lived in Brazil. I'd been in ads for a local department store and a health club. I was even Miss <u>Saude</u> Soda. But I was most popular in Brazil for hosting a teen television show called <u>Qual o lance?</u>, which means "What's Happening?" in Portuguese, the language we speak in Brazil. The show was about what's in style—you know, fashion, celebrities, and stuff. But that was all back in Rio. New York City is the big time! And Ford Models is about as big as you can get.

"...and, of course," Jerry was saying, "we have excursions and parties planned so that you can all get acquainted."

Great, I thought, I <u>love</u> parties. Back home in Rio, I went out just about every night. It was beginning to sound like this week would be pretty fun as well as help my career.

"Finally," said Eileen, "at the end of the week, one of you will be chosen to be Supermodel of the World. But all of you should be very proud. Simply having been chosen to represent your country in this contest means that each one of you is a winner already."

I guessed Eileen was right. It was nice to know that I'd been picked to go to the Supermodel Contest. But it wouldn't feel bad to win, either!

Well, I didn't win the contest, but I _was_ one of the seven finalists. Best of all, Ford took me on as one of their models!

I was heading to New York, the modeling center of the world! I'd shop at fashionable boutiques, go to exciting parties, and entertain glamorous friends in my own chic little apartment. I had it all planned out.

That is, until the Fords told me that they had arranged for me to stay in an apartment with a chaperone and five other girls they had brought to New York to model. It wasn't what I'd had in mind, but I wasn't about to argue. After all, the important thing was that I was on my way!

THE FORD SUPERMODELS OF THE WORLD COMPETITION

With branches in New York, Florida, Paris, Tokyo and Sao Paulo in Brazil, the Ford Agency is the largest and most prestigious modelling agency in the world. Famous names on the Ford books include Naomi Campbell, Christy Turlington, Christie Brinkley, Kelly Le Brock and Jerry Hall, while in the past, the agency has launched the careers of celebrities as well-known as Kim Basinger, Sharon Stone and Jane Fonda.

Constantly on the lookout for star quality in beautiful faces, the Ford family run an annual Supermodel of the World competition, open to all 14–24 year olds worldwide, in the hope of discovering the next international modelling superstar. The competition is sponsored by fashion magazines, cosmetic companies and TV shows all over the world, and the winner is guaranteed the leap from obscurity to the pinnacle of the world's most lucrative and glamorous career.

The next Supermodel of the World? As Eileen Ford says, "You never know at which bus stop, beach or barn dance she will show up. But you can be sure we're looking for her . . ."